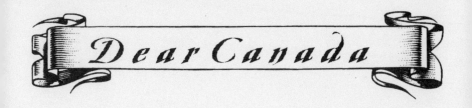

Winter of Peril

✦

The Newfoundland Diary of Sophie Loveridge

BY JAN ANDREWS

Scholastic Canada Ltd.

Deer Park, near Poole,
Dorset, England
March, 1721

Monday, March 6, 1721

I have hated writing these daily pages which Uncle Thaddeus has insisted upon, because I have never had ANYTHING to say. Now I have SOMETHING to say. But it scares me.

Mama and Papa and I are going away on a ship. It is Papa's idea. Mama is furious. But Papa has persuaded Uncle Thaddeus that it is what we must do.

I would put more but I do not know any more. I wish that someone would EXPLAIN.

Tuesday, March 7, 1721

The house is in an UPROAR. The packing has begun. Mama keeps to her bed.

At least I have found out why we are leaving. It is because Papa is going to be a poet and he believes "it is the work of a poet to chart new deeds." He also believes he will be like a man called Mr. Daniel Defoe, who wrote a book about another man who is called Robinson Crusoe who lived on an island all by himself.

Papa talked to me in the hallway after breakfast. Mostly what he wanted me to know is that by writing his own book he will become famous and make lots of money. I did not have to ask him why we need money. Have I not heard the servants whispering about how it is because he has none that we live here instead of in our own house?

Papa says Uncle Thaddeus has done all that he can "to thwart him in his purpose." But he has been "determined." I have known, of course, that something was afoot. I know always. But in this instance NO ONE would speak properly of it. Not even Nanny would do more than clasp me to her. "My poor little Mistress Sophie," she kept saying. But she did not say anything else.

Wednesday, March 8, 1721

Papa called me into the library. He unrolled a great map. I saw we are going to an island with *NEW FOUND LAND* written upon it.

But Newfoundland is where Uncle Thaddeus sends his fishing ships every summer! It is where he has told me hardly anyone lives.

In the nursery, Nanny started packing my silk gowns and my hooped petticoats into my trunk. Uncle Thaddeus brought other garments he said I would need. There is a common people's hooded cloak of red. There are bedgowns such as Nanny wears in the daytime and which wrap around. Linen caps and aprons. Wooden pattens to go over leather shoes upon my feet. Warm things to go under "for the months of winter." All are rougher than I am used to. I do not understand.

Thursday, March 9, 1721

Something has happened which feels as if it is going to be important.

I was in the schoolroom with Mistress Tyler. She was showing me a picture of Red Indians which she says "on my travels" I perchance may see. She wanted me to be "warned" for she says that the Red Indians are TERRIFYING.

Papa came. He took me in the carriage to the harbour to visit the ship that is called the *Daisy*, on which we will sail.

He said, YES, we are going to Newfoundland, but we are going to a part where "Mayhap no man of England e'er yet has set his foot." He told me we would not be coming back with the fishermen at the end of the summer.

I would have cried but Uncle Thaddeus appeared. He brought us to where there was an old man working with planks of wood all round him and a lovely round, red face.

Uncle Thaddeus said the man's name is Old Lige. It is strange to put this but Uncle Thaddeus made me think that with Old Lige I would be safe.

Friday, March 10, 1721

I have risen early because I HAVE TO get this down. Uncle Thaddeus has arranged that, when the ship comes home and we do not, Old Lige will stay there with us. Papa is angry but Uncle Thaddeus is insistent. He says *Robinson Crusoe* is a story and we are not.

He says that even now he could "return to his better judgment" and command the *Daisy* to sail without us. I wish that he would do this VERY MUCH.

Saturday, March 11, 1721

Mama has arisen. She is in a frenzy. The trunks have been taken away. Before they went, Uncle Thaddeus had Nanny put some of my clothes into a small bag to keep with me. I know I am supposed to be grown up but I have added my doll, Eliza. She is not very pretty but I have had her a very long time.

Sunday, March 12, 1721

There were prayers at church for "all the ships preparing to set forth." I prayed AS HARD AS I COULD. Uncle Thaddeus says we will set out ahead of most of the other shipping. That is because "all will be unfamiliar at the landing" and it may be necessary to search for a place with a good harbour and a beach "appropriate to the work."

Monday, March 13, 1721

I am on board, in the little cabin that apparently is to be mine. Uncle Thaddeus has introduced me to Captain Jones but we have not yet started on our voyage although the ship does move about.

I am writing because Uncle Thaddeus has given me a leather satchel with quills and ink and a blank book in it. Into the front of the blank book he has fixed all the pages I have written since I first found out Mama and Papa and I were leaving Deer Park.

Uncle Thaddeus says if I have what I have written right from the beginning, I will have the whole story — which he hopes I may find pleasing.

I do not know if I care about the whole story. I just know that using all these things makes Uncle Thaddeus seem a little near.

Saying goodbye to Nanny and to him was the worst thing that has ever happened to me. Even now, as I think about it, I find tears within my eyes.

Tuesday, March 14, 1721

I HATE it here. It is HORRIBLE. When we sailed it was late. No one came to undress me. I had to get under the covers with my gown still on. I am in it yet. I do not know how to get it off me.

A sailor called Jack visited this morning. He brought me a hard, HARD biscuit to eat with butter but I could not ask HIM. Mama and Papa do not come. Of course, they do not. I am supposed to have servants to look after me. Mama and Papa are supposed to have servants to look after them. Are there no servants here?

I would like to at least find where Mama and Papa are, but since we have been moving the shouting of men is doubled. Everything is creaking and shifting. I am frightened. When I try just to stand up, I cannot find my feet.

Later

Mama is in the cabin which is not next but the next after that. Papa took me to her. Mama has no one to help her either. She bid me tie the bows on the laces of her stays. I did not know how to do it. She became angry at my clumsiness. She sent me away.

I suppose my question about the servants is now answered. But having NO servants makes me feel more frightened still.

????

I do not know what day it is. I just know that I have been bringing up so often I think my whole insides of me have come out.

Saturday, March 18, 1721

I am feeling better. But then we are in a harbour once again. Captain Jones says we were "hit by a gale." We had reached somewhere called The Lizzard but were forced back to Plymouth, which is in Devon.

I have solved one of my problems. I tore my gown off me. Then, of course, I was worried. But I thought of Uncle Thaddeus and my small bag. I took one of the bedgowns to wear. I brushed my hair.

I am glad to get all this done because Jack has come to say that Captain Jones would like us to dine with him in his cabin. I am VERY HUNGRY INDEED.

Sunday, March 19, 1721

I have seen OLD LIGE!!! He was at the Sunday service, as Papa and I were. I hope God will not be angry that once I had seen Old Lige it was hard for me to think of anything else.

It was strange to have a service outside but there was a minister to conduct it. His name is Reverend Jacobs. He is the ship's chaplain. I could hardly hear the prayers because although we were going almost smoothly, the sails were flapping and waves were slapping at the sides.

The prayers did remind me it is Lent. They also reminded me I have not been attending to the Bible Nanny put in my small bag. I took my prayer book to the service, of course.

We dined with Captain Jones again. As well as Reverend Jacobs there was Mr. Chivers, who is something called a "boatswain," and Mr. Yonge, who is the surgeon to tend to everyone's health.

It is strange because we have to put the food onto our plates ourselves. Yesterday I did not know how to do this or how to pass the dishes when they came to me. Today I managed much better. And I was careful — just as Mistress Tyler had taught me for when I was dining with grown-up people (which of course I did only on special occasions at Deer Park). Listening to the grown-ups is interesting. Captain Jones told Papa we have to have a chaplain and a surgeon aboard "by law" because there are so many men. Mama asked Captain Jones if she might sit sometimes in his cabin because it is more spacious. He agreed but he said she must be careful not to touch his charts.

Sunday on the ship is not quiet as it is at home. I suppose that is because the ship cannot be stopped. It must go sailing on.

Monday, March 20, 1721

Captain Jones sent Jack to show me to Old Lige because I asked him. Old Lige was shaping a piece of wood. He told me it was to replace a part of the rigging that got damaged in the gale.

He said, "Begging your pardon, Mistress Sophie, but if ee will keep thy feet apart more, ee will find it better walking."

I was much more steady when I tried. Old Lige has a grandson on the ship. His name is Thomas. He is not the only boy aboard. There are others as well. Thomas has freckles and red hair. He showed me the smaller boats that are piled up wherever there is space. He said those are the boats the men will fish from and there will be five men for each boat. The fishing boats have no seats. The seats will be put in when we get there. Along with oars and other things.

It was strange simply to decide I wanted to see Old Lige and then to set out and do it. At home I would have had to ask permission. Mistress Tyler or Nanny would have gone with me. I did think about asking Mama or Papa, but then I thought how I have never really asked them about anything.

Being alone made me feel proud of myself.

Tomorrow I will put on the shoes and pattens Uncle Thaddeus gave me because I believe they will be more convenient. My silk shoes only get wet.

Tuesday, March 21, 1721

I went to see Old Lige again. I went everywhere. Whenever I got lost I walked until I was found. I met Peter, the cook, in his galley. I went to the hold where our trunks are. I saw a cow and a calf, some chickens and three small pigs. I also saw a cat but she ran away.

Pattens are not easy to walk in but I managed. I worked out for myself how it is necessary to almost slide my feet along.

I have many things to report. I have seen how the sails may be furled or unfurled depending on how fast we go. And how the steering is done by a wheel. By counting the fishing boats and then doing a sum, I discovered there are at least 100 men.

A SECRET. I have taken off my stays. I had not unloosed them before for fear I would not be able to retie them. I had worn them to bed even — as I did my gown at first. But I was so tired of their tightness. I undid them a little and then I could not bear to retie them. I do not think that I will put them on again.

Friday, March 24, 1721

I have not written for several days. I have been too busy.

But now we are in another harbour. It is called Waterford. Papa has taken Mama into the town "to view its wonders." We are stopped for provisions. They are being brought onto the ship as I write. One of the provisions is water. Also salt pork and salt beef, and cheese and butter. Everything is in barrels, or hogsheads. Old Lige says we have some things — such as peas and flour and the salt which is needed for the fishing in some way I do not understand yet — loaded already. He says whatever else we do not get, then we will have to go without.

We are also taking on more people. (Perhaps I was not right when I made my reckoning. Perhaps we are only arriving at 100 now.)

The people are Irish. They speak the Irish language — which is called Gaelic — as well as English. Among them there are two women. Old Lige says that is not as unusual as I thought.

Saturday, March 25, 1721

Captain Jones told me a most surprising thing. He said that although January 1 was the start of the "historical New Year" — and the New Year in many other places — in England the first day of the "Civil" or "Legal" year comes now. He called it the "actual year." This means that some people will have gone on writing 1720 until this very day. I asked him how it could be. He said it all has to do with Popes and history and who made up the calendars. He also told me "a seafaring man" — such as he is — knows there "be many different calendars" and many different times to start years out. Then he explained how he himself has been recording the date as 1720/21. I asked him if I should have done this. He said it is "not usual" when people are merely writing for themselves. I suppose I should also have asked him about that but I forgot.

Sunday, March 26, 1721

Some of the Irish people wanted to go to church instead of to Reverend Jacobs's service. Captain Jones would not let them. He says it is bad enough we must have PAPISTS aboard. He will not help them in their papish ways. I have never seen a papist so I studied them most particularly. I tried to see a difference but I could not.

Again Mama did not come to the service but later she did walk a little on the deck. She walked with Papa beside her and then she went in.

I have found out from Old Lige that the Irish women are called Katherine and Peg. Peg is the one who is shorter. Also I have found out that — when the Irish people speak English — it does not sound even like the men from Poole. The Poole speech is rounder and more rolling. The words of the Irish come like a flow.

The service set me to puzzling about how I am supposed to have given up something for Lent but how Lent is for things that are special. Here, we have that biscuit for breakfast and salt beef or pork with peas at midday and at dinner and sometimes pudding with plums. I think they are all what Mistress Tyler would call "staples." Although I suppose I have actually given up quite a lot just by coming on the *Daisy*. Even if I did not choose it.

I do not have the tea Mama and Papa have in the evenings because I do not like it. Tea is the most expensive of anything. Nanny told me. Captain Jones says the men drink cider with water and beer.

Perhaps it is wrong but at the service I prayed to God about the cat — if it is His will, of course. She rubs around Old Lige's legs so prettily. I would so much like her to rub around mine.

I am not going even to try to write every day any longer. There are too many interesting things to do.

P.S. I think the pattens are not as useful as Uncle Thaddeus thought they might be. They slip too easily. Perhaps they would be useful on land but not here. No one else has them. I shall not wear them any more.

Wednesday, March 29, 1721

We are sailing along the coast. I have seen hills and mountains. Captain Jones says "with current winds" we will have left Ireland behind us in two more days. I like Captain Jones. Today he told me why we have taken on the Irish people. He said it is because the Irish are poorer. He said in the last few years there has been less fish so the men from Dorset are not so willing to come. It is because of the less fish that Uncle Thaddeus is sending us exploring to the north once we reach Newfoundland. Apparently Uncle Thaddeus has "partners in this venture." Captain Jones says without partners the costs may be too high. What a very great deal to think about!

Friday, March 31, 1721

Old Lige showed me to the men who are the crew for his fishing boat. Their names are Rowlie and Aaron and Jim and Silas. When Silas speaks it makes me feel like laughing because he whistles through his teeth.

At dinner I noticed that Mama looks very fine still but Papa is more dishevelled. His wig is no longer powdered and he is growing a beard. Sometimes I have seen his shirt unbuttoned. I expect it is not polite for me to be noticing these things but how can I not?

Saturday, April 1, 1721

April Fool's Day. I did not do any jokes. Papa walked with me on the deck and Mama called me to read to her. I have never done jokes on them, however. And I was not sure whether it would be proper for me with anyone else.

The book Mama had chosen was a book of poetry. The poetry was by a man named Mr. Alexander Pope. The words were very hard. Mama was not pleased with me AGAIN.

The cat caught a mouse. Old Lige says that is why we have her. Otherwise we would be overrun.

Sunday, April 2, 1721

It is Palm Sunday. We had the Palm Sunday service although we were not given palm crosses to take away and keep beside us, as we are at home. Reverend Jacobs read about Jesus riding into Jerusalem on a donkey and how He was welcomed. I have always liked that story even if I know that what comes afterwards is so sad. I shall read it over for myself in my own Bible before I sleep.

Monday, April 3, 1721

A STORM. The waves are lashing. I am going to start bringing up again. I know it. The sea is too rough for me to write more.

Tuesday, April 4, 1721

The storm continues. I promised God I would read my Bible every day for Easter Week. I cannot. Not with how the ship is heaving. But so much now we need God's help.

Friday, April 7, 1721

Praise God, the storm is OVER and we have all survived. Sometimes I thought I would not. Especially when I was thrown out of my bunk and had to lie upon the floor. If I had not had Eliza to hold to me I do not know what I would have done.

Because it is Good Friday we have had a special Good Friday service of Holy Communion. Which I cannot take, of course, because I have not yet been confirmed. In his sermon, Reverend Jacobs told us to remember that what we have suffered is nothing compared to "the suffering of Our Lord."

Reverend Jacobs read about the Crucifixion but I shall read it over. I shall read all the pieces for Easter Week. I feel that perhaps I am only just beginning to understand what suffering is.

Saturday, April 8, 1721

I found out that, in the storm, one of the men fell and broke his leg so Mr. Yonge has had to set it. Mr. Yonge says he hopes the leg will mend well. I hope so too.

Also that some of the sails got torn. Jack is one of the sailors who is mending them. He showed me the thread he uses and how he greases it with beeswax so that it will run through. He let me try this contrivance that is called a "sailor's palm." It is made of leather and it helps him press in the needle. Mending sails is not like doing embroidery. I could not get the needle to move at all.

There is a boy on the ship who is not nice to me as everyone else is. His name is Joshua. This morning, it happened that I turned when I had gone past him. I saw that he was putting his thumb up to his nose. If his IMPERTINENCE occurs again then I will speak to Captain Jones about it so he will make it stop.

Sunday, April 9, 1721

Once more there was Holy Communion. I missed how the church would be all full of flowers for Easter Sunday. But I joined in the rejoicing nonetheless. I think Papa did too. Reverend Jacobs says we must "rejoice mightily." He says this day — when Our Lord is risen so others of us might overcome death and rise also — is the most, most JOYOUS DAY of all.

I walked with Thomas again. Thomas says he is surprised how, when there are no storms, the voyage "be full of dullness." I DO NOT think it is dull. I like watching. I like the sailors in the rigging best.

Monday, April, 10, 1721

Captain Jones is so kindly. He showed me what he calls the "ship's log." This is not a piece of wood but a record such as I am keeping. Only it is mainly about the weather.

The log says things like, "This morning the wind S.W., the sky full cloud."

The log "marks our course." This can be seen most clearly on the page where the dates are all set down upon one side and other titles along the top. The titles are for miles and something which is called our "latitude," which has to do with how far north or south we are. The number of miles is very variable. One day it was 41 and another only 9. Captain Jones says that these were "nautical miles," which are longer than miles on land. He said a "nautical mile" is 2026 yards of measure whereas a land mile measures only 1760 yards. I tried to do a sum to work out the difference — just for the 9 miles — but the sum was too hard.

Captain Jones seemed most surprised that I should want to know about such matters. He said most "of the fairer sex do not." Here is a strange thing though. Mama was in the cabin because she sits there always as Captain Jones has allowed her. I am certain she was listening even if she was pretending she was not.

Tuesday, April 11, 1721

I STEERED THE SHIP. It was only for a little but I did turn the wheel. I felt most powerful, standing holding it, with the wind blowing at me and salt spray coming on my lips. Captain Jones showed me his compass. Uncle Thaddeus has spoken to me already about how it is that a compass points the way. Captain Jones said always we must be going to the west. Then he said something which is a little scary. He said that although truly we know how far north or south we are, we do not know TRULY how far it is we have to go. That has do with our "longitude."

Captain Jones says there is no device yet "for the accurate measuring of it" for it has to do not only with miles travelled but with time. I think this means he does not quite know really where we are. He seemed, however, so confident that I tried to be confident as well.

Anyway, I was so INTERESTED. I wanted to learn more and more. Captain Jones gave me over to Mr. Chivers. I went with him to the back of the ship, which is the "stern." He showed me how the ship's speed is determined. This has to do with rope and knots and a glass for counting minutes and a sailor calling the answer aloud for all to hear.

Wednesday, April 12, 1721

Wind. Wind against us. Howling and roaring. I think we are still going forward but I am not certain. Captain Jones has ordered us all to keep to our cabins. He says it is not safe for us to go about. Again it is too rough to write more.

Thursday, April 13, 1721

Water has flowed in. It has wetted my bed linen. When Jack came I asked him if I might have some that is dry. He said that there is nothing dry "in all the ship."

Water has come into Mama's cabin also and into Papa's. Papa fears for his "creation" — his poem. He clutches the pages of it to him. Mama says we should fear rather for our lives.

At least now when the sea is rough I do not throw up. That is a mercy indeed.

Friday, April 14, 1721

There is fog. It swirls all round us. When I went out I could not see even to the end of the ship. What I did see is that everyone is listening for the sailor who is in the crow's-nest to call out that the way is clear.

Saturday, April 15, 1721

The fog continues. I continue wet. It is so long since I have seen Old Lige and Thomas that I am going to find them. Surely the fog cannot stop me. NOT IF I MAKE UP MY MIND.

Sunday, April 16, 1721

Old Lige brought me comfort. He told me of other voyages he has been on. He talked of how always he has returned to his "good missus" safe. When he found out my clothes were wet he sent Silas to fetch Katherine and Peg. They were very kind to me although I had not really met them before. They helped me dry my garments in Peter's galley by the stove.

The Sunday service seemed very strange because we could hardly see each other and because the fog makes everything so quiet. Mama still does not attend. Reverend Jacobs has suggested Papa might "lead her in her devotions," but I do not think she will be eager for that.

Monday, April 17, 1721

The wind is rising again. The fog has gone. Never before has the weather seemed to me important, as it does now.

Tuesday, April 18, 1721

We are on "cold rations." That is because it is too rough for Peter to cook.

Wednesday, April 19, 1721

Cold rations continue.

Saturday, April 22, 1721

Calmer. Captain Jones has said that soon I may begin looking for land. I am very excited, but I see nothing. What if the land is not there? What if we just have to keep sailing and sailing? I saw Mr. Chivers gazing out from the bow with a telescope so I went to him.

Mr. Chivers said, "There is much to be learned from waves and clouds."

The waves and clouds did not tell ME anything at all.

Sunday, April 23, 1721

St. George's Day. It does not always come on a Sunday, of course, but this time it has. Reverend Jacobs spoke of how St. George is the patron saint of England and how he slew the dragon. Reverend Jacobs said prayers for our arrival and that we might overcome "the demons that afflict us" in body, mind and soul. I have always liked to live in a country that has a dragon-slayer for a patron saint.

Again I looked for land. Captain Jones says we must also keep watch for ships from France because the French have "rights" in the regions where we are going. He says there is no war at the moment so we should not have any trouble, but that we can never be SURE.

Monday, April 24, 1721

I heard the cry, "Land ho!" I went running. I thought we would be safe but we are NOT. We are surrounded by ice chunks. We can see the land but we cannot reach it. Papa is suddenly exulting at the dangers. Captain Jones does not like this. Captain Jones is worried. Everyone else aboard is also. More than they have ever been. Captain Jones has ordered Mama and Papa and me to stay below again. He says the ice can trap us. The chunks are so big. I see them through the little porthole. One rose up. It crashed against the ship's side. At this moment, we are held unmoving. I am going to read in my Bible where Jesus calmed the waves.

Tuesday, April 25, 1721

I disobeyed Captain Jones. I went from my cabin. I tried to go onto the deck. But there is ice there too. It is formed from the sea's spray. It is all over. Even in the rigging.

The men are trying to melt it. They are boiling water in pots and kettles. They are trying to use the steam. They are hacking at the ice with axes. I heard someone say that with all the ice upon it the ship cannot be steered. I went to tell Mama.

Mama said a terrible thing to me.

She said, "At least if the ship goes down our torment will be at an end."

I do not want the ship to go down. I want to get where we are going. Wherever it is will be safer than where we are now. Uncle Thaddeus was right. We should not EVER, EVER have set out.

Birds are on the ice. Seagulls. They cry and clamour. There are other birds too. Some smaller black and white ones. Jack says they are called "sea pigeons." I think how they can fly and we cannot.

Jack comes to see that all is well with me. He tells me Newfoundland "be the most unpredictable place" for weather in all the world.

Thursday, April 27, 1721

I heard a great cheer. I rushed to the porthole. I saw that we are in clear water. I shall go out and see how this may be.

Friday, April 28, 1721

We have LAND! Land to our left (which Captain Jones has told me over and over I must call "to port"). What does it matter what I call it? I can see it. We are in a channel that is open. Ice is to our right still but LAND IS TO OUR LEFT.

Saturday, April 29, 1721

We go slowly because we must take "soundings." That is because we do not want to "run aground." It is still treacherous on the deck but once more I have been there. I have seen how the rope for the soundings is lowered over the side and how the rope has marks for measurements. The measurements are in "fathoms." I hear the sailor calling the fathoms out — so Captain Jones will know them — even now.

Sunday, April 30, 1721

We are in a cove. Captain Jones has declared it "more than suitable." The men are fitting out several of the fishing boats so that they may row unto the land. I do not want to go. There are too many trees and it is dark beneath them. The trees make me remember about the Red Indians.

All of a sudden I am like Mama. Mama says she would not "willingly set foot within this dreadful place, for all the riches in the world."

Reverend Jacobs's service was one of thanksgiving. I did not know how to be thankful. I am too afraid.

Monday, May 1, 1721

I was mean. I did not put how glad the men all are to be here. I can put that now because I see that those who went to the land have come back SAFE. I want to go too. I want to go dearly. I shall find Captain Jones and speak to him of this.

Still, it is strange to be here. At home on the first of May it is so much warmer. On village greens, there is dancing. Uncle Thaddeus takes us in the carriage to watch. Dancing here is impossible. Except for the beach, there is no clear space.

Tuesday, May 2, 1721

The land was too steady. I could not walk upon it. Thomas said he had the same trouble. He said Old

Lige had told him, after a voyage, "'Tis so always."

I came back early with Peter and Katherine and Peg. I did that because the land still scared me a little. Now, I wish that I had stayed. When we were on the land I met Katherine and Peg's husbands. Peg's husband is named Aengus and Katherine's is called Eamon. Eamon especially did not seem very pleased to see me. He has red hair like Thomas's but his eyes are green.

On the land, I had to be careful. The men are chopping the trees down. The trees fall with great crashes. The crashes shake the ground.

There was also snow in patches. The snow was quite dirty. It did not look nice at all.

Wednesday, May 3, 1721

How BRAVE I am getting! I went exploring. ALL BY MYSELF. I found out the forest is not scary, it is interesting. And it smells nice. And the wind sounds whispering within the trees. After I had finished being in the forest I went to the stream. I saw that beyond it there is another, second beach. It is like the beach where the men are working, for there are stones upon it. Behind the beach a hill goes rising. The hill has no trees upon it but there are many rocks and small, low plants.

I did not stop by the stream. I CROSSED IT. Thomas came to get water. He showed me how to cross by going from rock to rock. I got my feet wet but it was only a little. And when they were wet I did not care!

Afterwards I went with him to where he was working with Old Lige. They were not chopping the trees down. They were cutting off the branches. Old Lige says the trees are to build things but he did not say what.

Papa went upon the land also. For him, it was the first time. He said that before, he had been too busy setting down all "such delights" as he could see. Even today he did not stay long. He is so very eager always to be at his writing work.

Friday, May 5, 1721

Already the forest is farther away. I had to walk through stumps to get to it. Papa speaks of "the empire of England a-building" and how perhaps he will start "a plantation," which he says is like "founding a colony." Does that mean he thinks we will stay here forever? He does muddle me up.

Here is something I found out. There are to be "stages" for us to walk upon so we will not always have to go to the land by boat. The *Daisy* will "sit at" one and there will be two others. Already the men have begun to set up the posts.

I suppose I should also put that I stayed on the land and ate my midday meal with Old Lige. And with the others of his crew. I think I would like to do that always now.

Sunday, May 7, 1721

Reverend Jacobs has decreed that, since we have arrived, the Lord's Day must be kept "as well as may be managed." That means that he had a service in the evening as well as the morning and that the men did no work.

Ice has come into the cove. The wind has blown it. Joshua and Thomas and some of the other boys went out upon it. They chased each other from chunk to chunk. Captain Jones was angry with them. He says we have done well that no one has drowned so far and he does not want anyone drowning now. I told Thomas he should not have gone there — ESPECIALLY ON A SUNDAY. Thomas just laughed.

Monday, May 8, 1721

It is raining. Captain Jones told me not to go upon the land, but I went and then everyone was busy and I had to wait for a boat to bring me back. I got so wet and cold I started shivering. Now I look out and see everything dripping and streaming and I feel something inside me that I do not understand.

I think it is a horror such as Mama continues to feel in this new place here. But the horror was not with me yesterday when the rain was not upon us. It is very disturbing. I am finding that when I want to go home to Deer Park I feel I am like Mama and when I am happy here I feel I am like Papa again. Almost I am like two people and not me at all.

The men work on, but surely, SURELY, they cannot like being cold and wet either. Surely some of them must feel about it as I do.

Tuesday, May 9, 1721

I have come to a decision. I have decided I want to be USEFUL. I have been pacing my cabin as Mama does. I want to be useful because I want Old Lige to smile at me as he smiles when Thomas brings him a log or something and he says to Thomas, "Ee art a useful lad."

Wednesday, May 10, 1721

At dinner Captain Jones spoke of how the men are making houses to live in that are called "tilts."

He told Mama and Papa he has been worrying about this because the tilts "be built so small."

Mama said she would remain upon the ship. Papa said, of course, he would stay with her "for her protection." He was most gallant about it. Neither of them spoke of what would happen to me. They did not seem to think about it. I suppose, truly, they are so used to having Uncle Thaddeus look out for me and also make sure that the servants do likewise, that they believe that somehow he is doing this still.

Anyway, Captain Jones seemed to assume that I would stay upon the ship if Mama and Papa were doing so. I suppose then that I will.

Friday, May 12, 1721

The stage for the *Daisy* is finished. I have walked upon it. It is made of logs set close together. The logs do not fit tight to each other so when I looked down between them I could see the sea.

As soon as the last nail was put in, the animals were brought out. Jack brought the chickens. He held them by their feet so their heads were dangling. They did not seem to mind at all. Aengus brought the cow and the calf, which is much grown now. Katherine and Peg helped him. The cow and the calf both struggled and bellowed. The pigs were also a trouble. They are also grown. It was Joshua's father who worked mostly with them. He is called Amos. I had thought that Joshua was here alone but now I know that he is not. His father treated the animals very roughly. He shouted a great deal.

Peter says mostly the animals have been brought because Mama and Papa and I are staying. Otherwise, he says, for certain there would be no calf and no pigs.

Captain Jones says that "only a portion of the stage construction is accomplished." The men must now set up a roof on the part that is closest to the land and make tables to go under where the roof is. It is a little complicated because in fact it is where the roof and the tables are that is really the stage part. The part that stretches ahead of that — further over the water — is called the stage head.

Here is something else. The *Daisy* has been un-rigged and the masts lowered. Captain Jones says this is so the ropes and sails may be better protected from the weather "all the summer long."

Sunday, May 14, 1721

I still want to be USEFUL and so I prayed for that.

Monday, May 15, 1721

God has answered my prayers. I was USEFUL to Peter. I carried an egg for him. I brought it from the little house where the chickens are living to the cook-room that has been built for him. I set it on the table, safe.

Peter is making something that is called "spruce beer." He has put branches into water that is in barrels. He says he will show me the beer's progress. He also says the beer is most important for it keeps folks "in good health" and the cider will soon run out.

Tuesday, May 16, 1721

The chickens laid two eggs. I carried both of them. Peter showed me how to get them out of the nest, even. To reach in under where the chickens are sitting. Peter says I may be his helper when the chickens are let out to roam in the forest "if I wish it."

I wish it and wish it — VERY MUCH.

Nothing has happened to the spruce beer yet. Peter says it will not for one more day.

Eamon and Aengus have started working on one of the tilts. Katherine and Peg are spending much time with them. When they are all of them together they laugh A GREAT DEAL.

Wednesday, May 17, 1721

The hens are growing used to me. Especially the speckled one. She cocks her head in a very nice way when I come.

Papa was walking ashore and so I took him to see them. He called them "our feathered friends." I did not tell him about my egg collecting. It is hard for me to admit this but, more and more, I am certain that if Mama and Papa knew what I was doing they would say it is not proper "for a lady." I know I should think on this but I do not want to, so I will say no more.

I tasted the spruce beer. Peter says I will get used to it. I hope that this is true.

Friday, May 19, 1721

Reverend Jacobs said prayers for Ascension Day when Jesus was finally taken up to Heaven.

There was so much rain Peter said I should not go for the egg bringing. I have to admit I was not sorry. Perhaps I should have been. Perhaps I should have argued. After all, everyone else keeps working on and on.

Sunday, May 21, 1721

The chickens are let out. Peter was right when he said the egg bringing would be harder. I had to watch them carefully to see where they might go. Still, I got eight eggs for my trouble. Peter says the chickens will return to their house at night and he will shut them in "for fear of foxes." I had not thought of foxes. I wonder — if I should come upon one — if it would bite.

Peter says the chickens must be let out so they can peck in the earth and get food for themselves. He says the pigs will be tied to stakes for the same reason although they will also be given what is left over from the men's meals. He is worried about the cow and calf. He says the pigs will root in the earth but the only place where there is any sort of grazing for cattle is upon the hill across the stream and that looks "mean and sparse." Uncle Thaddeus sent extra hay but that is for the winter. And Peter does not think it is enough.

Peter is very insistent that the animals must be cared for — SUNDAYS OR NO.

Monday, May 22, 1721

Old Lige has taken me inside the tilt that he and Thomas and Aaron and Rowlie and Silas and Jim are making. He has told me that they will put bits of bark inside it to line it. The bark is called "rinds" and the rinds will be nailed on. I asked him why, on the tilts that are finished, there is earth put in great chunks upon the roofs. He said it is to help keep the warmth in and the rain out. There are rinds under the earth on the roofs for that as well.

A tilt has only one room to it. And the floor is just the ground. I think Mama is right to keep her cabin on the *Daisy*. A tilt is VERY DIFFERENT from Deer Park.

As the tilts get finished the men move into them. Old Lige says he and his crew will move tomorrow but already it is quiet and more lonely aboard.

Wednesday, May 24, 1721

Captain Jones and Mr. Chivers and Reverend Jacobs and Mr. Yonge have also "repaired to the land."

Now that Mr. Chivers is gone, our trunks have been brought up and set in his cabin. At first I was very excited, but when the lids were opened I found that everything within was damp. I would have been quite downcast, but then I remembered how sometimes when Katherine and Peg were on the ship still they would put clothes upon a line to air and dry. I found the line and I used it. I actually took some of Papa and Mama's clothes also. When I brought the clothes in they smelled much better. I could hardly wait to get on a new bedgown — which I am wearing even now.

For the first time, Peter did not cook upon the ship but in a cook-room on the shore. He does not have a stove there but a fire. He says the fire means more bending, which he could "do without."

Despite the changes, we still dined with Captain Jones in his cabin. Peter cooked on land and the food was brought.

Here is THE BEST THING. The cat has come to be with me. She is even letting me stroke her. Old Lige says she does not have a name so I am calling her Tibbles because I remember Nanny telling me she had a cat called Tibbles once.

I miss talking to Nanny. Sometimes I even miss Mistress Tyler's lessons. Although I do not miss them quite so much.

Sunday, May 28, 1721

This is not just any Sunday. It is Whit-Sunday. When Reverend Jacobs read the part from The Acts of the Apostles about the Day of Pentecost, I found I was saying the words over. That is because Mistress Tyler had me learn them so I could recite them by heart.

Friday, June 2, 1721

I should have written sooner about how there are rack things being built with spruce boughs spread on them. The racks are called "flakes." Thomas says they are to dry the fish on. He is very excited. He talks about the fishing a GREAT DEAL.

I think he would like to be going out in the fishing boat with Old Lige, but he has told me he will not be able to do this. He says Aaron and Jim will not go either because, in each crew, "there be need of some to work ashore."

Monday, June 5, 1721

I stayed in my cabin and held Eliza because I was not feeling very well. Captain Jones noticed. He came to visit me. He asked me what was the matter. I said I did not know. It was very good of him to come when he has so much else to be concerned with. He sent Jack to bring me some soup. Papa came also. He said he wished "to note our vicissitudes." I did not like that.

I am sure that tomorrow I will be feeling better. Perhaps I have had what Mistress Tyler used to call "the vapours." Although I think "the vapours" has to do with fainting. I did not FAINT at all.

Tuesday, June 6, 1721

I was right. I am better. I could spend all day on the land again.

Wednesday, June 7, 1721

Right when I set out from the ship I saw that the sea close to the shore was "broiling" — as I think Papa might say. I ran. I found the water full of little silver fishes. Old Lige says they are called "capelin" and they will be used as bait. It is the job of the boys to catch the capelin in baskets that are called "maunds." A maund is like a sieve. It is dipped into the water. The capelin are held in it and the water runs through. Thomas took me to show me all about it. He waded out, dipped his maund and brought it back so I might see. I did not wade out for I did not know what I would do if my skirts became soaked through.

There are places on the beach where the capelin that have got washed up are so many they can be gathered with the hands. The boys did that as well.

The gulls come for the capelin also. They scream and wheel. We had fried capelin for dinner. Tibbles liked it too.

Thursday, June 8, 1721

I HATE Joshua. He has spoiled EVERYTHING. Again I was watching Thomas get capelin. Joshua started teasing him. He said I was Thomas's sweetheart. Thomas dropped his maund and ran away.

I have not even ever thought of having "a sweetheart." And is not Thomas one of the common people? Do I not know a common person cannot be a sweetheart for me?

Friday, June 9, 1721

Thomas has a black eye but Joshua has one that is blacker and his lip is split as well. I do not think I will write any more because there is something frightening to me in all this.

Luckily Tibbles is here and she is purring. The purring is a very soothing sound.

Saturday, June 10, 1721

The boys continue to catch capelin. They spread them on the shore to dry. I do not go to be near Thomas. I do not want Joshua talking of sweethearts EVER AGAIN.

Sunday, June 11, 1721

Trinity Sunday. I prayed that Thomas's eye would get better. I do not like him to be hurt. Before the service this morning, Captain Jones announced that the fishing will start in just four days. He asked that we pray for "success in our venture." I did that also. In the morning and in the evening. I shall do so again before I sleep.

Thursday, June 15, 1721

The fishing boats went out while I was still sleeping. They went long before the dawn. We waited until almost dark. But the boats came back EMPTY.

Old Lige says, "Perhaps t'will be better tomorrow."

I hope so much that this is so.

For the fishing the men wear special aprons. The aprons are made of sheepskin. The leather side is outside and it is covered in tar. Jim says the aprons are for keeping dry and warm "as well as might."

Friday, June 16, 1721

Aaron has told me how to know "the outcome of the day" from whether the fishing boats "be lower in the water" and whether the men "be leaning more upon their oars." I did not have to look for those things. I could tell from the men's faces, which were so solemn and so sad.

Saturday, June 17, 1721

Captain Jones is trying to convince the men that perhaps "our more northerly clime" is affecting us so that the fish will not come "at the customary date." I do not think the men believe this. After the fishing boats came in I heard Joshua's father muttering to Jack about how maybe we have come to the wrong place. And how now "it be too late to start over." Joshua's father was very angry. His voice made shivers in my spine.

Sunday, June 18, 1721

Because it is Sunday, the men did not go out upon the water. We prayed FOR FISH.

Monday, June 19, 1721

The boys have stopped collecting bait. Thomas says they believe "it be no use." As we waited for the fishing boats' return, Thomas sat beside me. I saw Joshua looking at him and I saw Thomas looking back with what I think was a proud look on his face. I will admit that I was proud myself.

Here is something I DO NOT UNDERSTAND. When I try to explain to Mama and Papa about what is happening, Mama takes no notice and Papa talks of how the important time is not now — the important time will begin when we are alone here after everyone else has left.

I suppose he says that because then we will be more like Robinson Crusoe. But today when I was with Katherine and Peg THEY said that if the fish do not come the men will make no money and their families will starve. I know when I was at home I did not care about fish and I did not know about people starving, but I am different here. I think of how even Uncle Thaddeus will surely suffer.

The worst time is when the fishing boats return. Old Lige comes last always. Thomas says that is because Old Lige "be not a one for giving up."

Tuesday, June 20, 1721

THE FISH STILL DO NOT COME. And there is something else that is HORRIBLE. Thousands of little flies swarm. They are called blackflies and they bite. I was tempted to tell Peter I could not collect eggs for fear of them. But he is always so pleased when I do it and his pleasedness makes me glad.

The boys have made smoky fires to keep the blackflies away but the fires do not work. As I was egg-searching my hands and face grew covered. Now I am itching and itching. One of my eyes is swollen so that it is almost shut.

Wednesday, June 21, 1721

I heard this cry. The fishing boats WERE low in the water. Old Lige and Rowlie and Silas and the others WERE pulling much, much harder on the oars.

The fishing boats did not land on the beach. They went to the ends of the stage heads. Everyone was shouting. I wanted to shout also. So I did. A man jumped off first in each boat to "brew a kettle" for the others. In Old Lige's boat it was Rowlie. Aaron went running up to him. He slapped him on the back.

The men in the fishing boats were standing with fish up to their knees. The fish were writhing and heaving. The men used these spear things. They started throwing the fish up. The fish were so many they looked like rain. It is the boys who must catch the fish. And the fish must be split upon tables. But everything was happening so quickly I could not understand it. I just know that the split fish are let fall onto what Captain Jones told me are called "drooge barrows" and that the drooge barrows are carried away by two men holding the poles. The fish are then put in piles with salt and the piles are called "salt bulk." That is what the salt we brought in the *Daisy* is for.

Before I knew it the piles were higher than my chest and they got higher still. Everything became very messy, but I did not mind it. I did not mind it either that Captain Jones suggested I might leave because soon there would not be any room for me to stand.

The men work on. They work by lantern light. How good that it is midsummer's day when in England again there would be dancing. Surely, in our hearts, we all are dancing here!

Thursday, June 22, 1721

Fish and more fish! The men went out and came back and went out again. Each time the boats were loaded.

Papa bid me walk with him. We crossed the stream though he is not so good at it as I am. We went past the cow and the calf. We climbed up onto the clifftop where I have never been. I was able to look down and see the fishing boats below us. I watched how the men throw out the long lines with hooks on. And how they have to haul on the lines to get the fish up. I saw how — because each line has other lines that are called "snoods" attached to them — the men can catch several fish at once.

Old Lige sits in the back of his boat. That is because he is "the master" and it is he who steers. Silas and Rowlie are "midshipman" and "foreship-man." They sit side by side and they face him. They cannot see where they are going at all. I have found out that the fish the men are really seeking is a fish that is called cod fish. I waved to Old Lige but he did not see me. If he had I know he would have waved back.

I have been so excited about the fish I have not put how the blackflies continue. Captain Jones has had Peg show me how to tie a piece of cloth over my cap and around my head and neck so it is harder for them to get in. Katherine has given me some grease to smear upon my face and hands. I am still VERY BITTEN.

Everyone else is also. Even the animals. I am reminded of the plague of flies that God sent upon the Egyptians in the Bible. I have never been sorry for the Egyptians before, but I am now.

Friday, June 23, 1721

I ran to the end of the stage head to see Old Lige when he came in. He told me the men who open the fish up with a knife by cutting along the bellies are called "cut throats."

"Watch how the cut throats do give the fish to the headers," he said.

Even I did not have to ask what the "headers" do. They cut off the fish heads. The "splitters" take out the backbone. They are the ones who make the fish flat.

The fish insides are thrown down holes in the stages to fall into the sea. Except for the livers. They are dropped into tubs which are called "train vatts." I realize now I should have asked Old Lige what the livers are for. I forgot because Old Lige wanted to show me how the men who put the salt on for the salt bulk with brushes and wooden shovels must be careful. They must use just the right amount of salt or the fish will spoil.

Aaron is a header and Jim is a splitter. It is no wonder that, without Old Lige, I could not understand what was happening. He told me that almost five hundred fish may be split by one man in just one half an hour.

Because of the fish, more flies have come. They

are called bluebottles. They do not bite but they land on everything and they buzz.

Saturday, June 24, 1721

Fog. The men were out when it came down. Two of the fishing boats did not return. One of the boats has Joshua's father in it. Mr. Chivers took a party to the clifftop. They lit a fire. They shouted and shouted. At least that is what Thomas tells me. I stayed with Katherine and with Peg.

Sunday, June 25, 1721

The fog persists. Many of the prayers at Reverend Jacobs's services were prayers for rescue. The other boats have gone out looking. That is something that can be done on Sundays, and it MUST.

I am frightened for Old Lige — and Silas and Rowlie, of course. Katherine and Peg are frightened for their men too. They clutched at their shawls. Thomas and Joshua and two of the other boys have been keeping the fire on the clifftop burning. But even from the beach it seems only a glimmer.

The men that were in one of the boats are called Randall and Samuel and Titus. The men that were in the other — with Joshua's father — are Andrew and Jacob. Thomas says Joshua is pretending not to care because his father is mostly only angry with him. Can he truly not want his father to return?

Monday, June 26, 1721

In the night I heard the wind rise. At first I was pleased because Aaron had told me it is wind that blows the fog away. But the wind blew into a storm. None of the fishing boats went out. The sea is too rough for them. But what of the boats that are out there? With all the rain, the fire on the clifftop has gone out.

Tuesday, June 27, 1721

One of the fishing boats that was lost is found. It is the boat that belonged to Randall and Samuel and Titus but there is no one in it. Old Lige says the boat that carried Joshua's father and Andrew and Jacob is "most like broken up upon some rock." There is no searching any longer. Captain Jones says there is no longer hope.

There is another plague. This time it is of mosquitoes. Katherine has given me some ointment she says is made from the buds on poplar trees. The mosquitoes bite also. Are they like a DOOM?

Wednesday, June 28, 1721

Reverend Jacobs held a funeral for the men. He committed the souls of those who have been lost unto God. He said how their bodies would be resurrected like the "glorious body" of Jesus. Tears came into my eyes. Katherine and Peg were crying as well. When it was all over Joshua went and threw stones into the sea.

Papa said the service was "most affecting." Mama did not come. I have never known anyone to die before. I tried to look upon Joshua kindly but he looked upon me only with scorn.

Thursday, June 29, 1721

I did not think that everything could go back to being normal, but it has. The boats set out again before the dawning and so the work goes on.

Here is what I have found out about the fish. The split fish in the salt bulk piles must be "saved." This does not mean they will be rescued. It means they will be "preserved."

They stay in the salt bulk only "a certain time." That time depends upon the weather. For now it has been seven days, but it might be four or nine.

After the salt bulk fish are ready, they are washed by the boys in the sea or in the stream. When the washing is done, the fish are piled on what are called "horses" made of beach stones. The boys started upon this today.

The washing is like a whole new beginning because after it the fish must be spread out upon the flakes. That will start tomorrow. Katherine and Peg will work at the spreading. So will some of the men left on the land when the fishing boats go out. Thomas was right when he told me the spreading is so that the fish may dry. I shall, of course, go to see how it is done.

Captain Jones says the flakes are still "not the end of the matter." When the time on the flakes is done, the fish will be put into "prest piles." There the salt will be "sweated out" of them — whatever that might mean.

After the prest piles the fish will be spread on the ground. The boys will do this also. They will leave the fish on the ground for one more day. The fish will then be put in "dry piles." By doing a sum, I worked out that it will be AT LEAST two to three weeks from when the fish are caught till when they are ready for the dry piles. This means it is two to three weeks before they are ready to be sold.

I told Captain Jones about my sum. He smiled at me. He said I may be right in my answer, but then he said also that the weather can make "a vast deal of difference" to it all.

What a lot of new words to remember. And a lot of things that need to happen to the fish. I was afraid I might not be able to set it down properly as Captain Jones informed me, but I think I have.

P.S. It was good to do a sum again. I have not done one for ages. Uncle Thaddeus was always so insistent as to how Mistress Tyler should teach me. And I like how the numbers come in my head.

Saturday, July 1, 1721

Again Joshua has been CRUEL to me. All I did was remark to Katherine how the fish on the flakes look so different — not like the living fish at all.

He muttered to Peg so I could hear him.

He said, "Has her got nothing better to do than to be getting in our ways?"

I left because my tummy felt cold and empty and I wanted to cry.

Sunday, July 2, 1721

I did not go to the services. I pretended I did not feel well again. I prayed by myself. I prayed for Joshua to go away.

The "shore work" continues even though it is Sunday. I heard Captain Jones telling Papa about it.

He said if the fish are not cared for they may spoil, and surely God must know of this.

Monday, July 3, 1721

Again all day I have kept to the *Daisy*. I have clutched Eliza to me and been sad. I SHOULD speak to Captain Jones about Joshua, but I have this idea that Thomas would not like it and so I do not.

Tuesday, July 4, 1721

I decided I would not "get in the way" any longer. I would WORK as others do. I asked Katherine and Peg if I might help them and they said I might.

Spreading the fish is harder than it looks because the fish are heavy and I am only just tall enough to reach. I could not work all day but I did work part of it. Katherine and Peg said I did a good job. Thomas looked approvingly at me. I liked that.

Wednesday, July 5, 1721

Today is rainy. That means the fish cannot be put out. I am not sorry. From what I did yesterday my hands are quite, quite SORE.

Mama has found her watercolour paints and brushes in her trunk. She has started on a picture. It seems much rougher than other pictures of hers that I have seen. Now that the men are gone from the *Daisy* she walks out here often in good weather. Mostly she walks by herself, though sometimes with Papa.

Thursday, July 6, 1721

I worked with Katherine and Peg again but I am worried. I know that ABSOLUTELY, DEFINITELY Mama would not approve. (Papa might not say anything but it would only be because he was not paying attention!!)

That is not even everything.

I see that my egg collecting was so little. I see it has to be done, but anyone else would do it as if it were nothing and then go on to something more. I do not know if I can I be like that. I do not know what will happen to me if I can.

Am I not SUPPOSED to be a lady?

Does that not mean I am not supposed even to WANT to work?

Friday, July 7, 1721

Here is something else. This morning I grew thirsty. I wanted to ORDER Peg to bring me some water. I did not do so because something inside me told me it would make everything different.

Mama would have ordered. SHOULD I have done so?

I have tried talking to Eliza and to Tibbles about all this but, of course, they do not answer. God does not either. Not in any way that seems clear.

Sunday, July 9, 1721

Papa came to fetch me where I was working. Katherine and Peg curtseyed to him as they always do. Papa and I went once more onto the clifftop. The sea was full of these things that are called icebergs. Some of them were as big as the *Daisy* almost. Old Lige says they will be in the water for a time now and then they will be gone. He says the men must be careful fishing near them for they can turn over and a nearby boat will be swamped.

I think the icebergs have blue parts in them. I would like to see what the blue parts are.

Sometimes I feel like Thomas. I wish I could be out in the fishing boats with Old Lige and Silas and Rowlie. I wish it VERY MUCH.

Monday, July 10, 1721

The weather is beautifully warm and pleasant. Katherine has given me a kind of ointment for my sore hands. She says even hands such as hers are "a terrible trouble to her" in such times.

I have found out that the cod livers are put in the vatts because they turn into oil, which is sold.

The pigs were squealing A LOT today but I do not know why.

Tuesday, July 11, 1721

Another man has been lost. He is Jack's cousin. His name is Ned.

Old Lige told me what happened. Ned's foot was caught in the fishing line and he was pitched into the sea. The others in the boat tried to help him but because his clothing was wet he was too heavy and their hands gave way.

Captain Jones has asked Old Lige if he will make some crosses. He says he has decided that even if the men who are lost cannot be buried, "their passage should not go unmarked."

Wednesday, July 12, 1721

Another funeral. Reverend Jacobs asked us to pray that there "might be no more." I did that, of course. Old Lige has put up the crosses in a place at the edge of the forest. They look very sad.

The men have started using "jiggers" for bait

now. Silas showed me. A jigger is a metal thing that is shaped like a fish and has hooks on it. It must be moved up and down.

Thursday, July 13, 1721

Suddenly the sun is beating hot. Thomas and the other boys must come more often with the water buckets. And with Peter's spruce beer. I tried taking my shoes off because the boys go barefoot often. I liked it although I could not stay thus very long because the beach stones hurt my feet.

Something GOOD. Peg said I might help her and Katherine with the piles they must make from the fish that are drying, whenever it is raining, and at night. These piles are called "faggots." They are important. Because I have been watching I knew just how to set the fishes — with the skins upwards and with bigger fish on top so that "any damp might be kept out." Peg said I had done well.

Mostly when I am working with Katherine and Peg they talk in English but sometimes they talk in Gaelic. And sometimes now I seem to understand.

Friday, July 14, 1721

Mama is sick. I was going by her cabin and I heard her moaning. I went in and tried to hold her hand but she snatched it away. Mr. Yonge is with her now. Katherine and Peg are there also. Mr. Yonge has said Mama should have those to care for her who are "from the female side."

Saturday, July 15, 1721

Katherine and Peg stay all the time. Mr. Yonge comes and goes. He says Mama is hotter. Papa and I are prevented from entering her cabin. But I think Mama is bleeding. I have seen the blood upon the sheets set down outside her door.

Sunday, July 16, 1721

Something happened in the night.

Peg says, "'Tis called a miscarriage."

Katherine says, "Your mother was to have a baby and now she will not."

I do not know what "miscarriage" means. I do not know where babies come from. I asked Nanny once. She told me babies were to be found "at the bottom of the garden." I looked, but there were none. Anyway, now I think about it, I know Nanny's voice had a funny sound to it. As if she were not telling me the truth.

Mr. Yonge says Mama must continue resting. Katherine may return to work but Peg must remain.

I do not think Papa has been told about the baby, for I heard Mr. Yonge saying "the dear lady's troubles are for women's ears alone."

Monday, July 17, 1721

I have been to see Mama and she looks very pale. I wish that SOMEONE would tell me about the baby that was coming. I wish it A GREAT DEAL.

Tuesday, July 18, 1721

Mama seems much better. She even had me brush her hair. She complained when I pulled at the tangles. Peg has returned to work. It is Papa who attends upon Mama. I do not expect I should put this, but I have found out that it is he who helps her dress.

Wednesday, July 19, 1721

I went back to work. Everyone was pleased to see me. The men had heard of Mama's illness although they did not know its nature, of course. Lots of them told me they wished her "good health."

I notice now that there are piles of fish all over. Some of the fish is "finished." It is in the "dry piles." The dry piles are covered with rinds.

Thursday, July 20, 1721

Mama continues to get better. She has had Papa read to her from Alexander Pope. Also she came again to dinner. Papa had to help her, but she did.

Friday, July 21, 1721

I am so upset. My head is full of going to and fro. When dinner was done Captain Jones asked Papa to walk upon the deck with him. I know it was not right but I suspected something important was going to happen. And no one ever tells me ANYTHING until it is too late. I went up to listen from where I could not be seen.

I heard Captain Jones saying that soon a "sack ship" will come to take away the fish that is ready. It will not go straight to England but it will go there soon. He asked if — in light of Mama's "most recent illness" — Papa would like to take the opportunity to leave.

For a moment I was so happy — just to think of being at Deer Park again. Of not having to work hard any longer. Of never being worried and wet. Then I thought how I would not see Thomas and Old Lige and Peter and Katherine and Peg and all the others. My heart sank down within me.

Mama knows none of this. Of course I cannot tell her, for I am not supposed to know.

Saturday, July 22, 1721

Still, Papa has not spoken to Mama about our leaving. He talks only of his plans. He has even said that he and Mama must take me as an example of "resourcefulness." It did not make her look more kindly upon me. Did he expect it would?

And is it good to be RESOURCEFUL? What will Uncle Thaddeus say when he finds out? Will he be angry? Will he say it is not fitting? What if when he discovers I have been working he does not want me to be with him at Deer Park anymore?

All day I kept looking to see if a ship was coming. I even went onto the clifftop. I want so much to talk to Old Lige or Katherine or Peg or SOMEONE!! But I CANNOT.

Sunday, July 23, 1721

Mama has learned of the ship. She is arguing with Papa this very minute. At the services I tried to pray for a happy conclusion to our family's difficulties. But I do not know what that would be.

Monday, July 24, 1721

The ship has come. I did not see Mama's face when it arrived, but I can imagine it. She seems so happy. She seems not to believe that Papa will not let us depart.

Uncle Thaddeus sent me a letter. It told of how he misses me. It made me think of Nanny and I wanted to weep. I am not going to put any more because I am going to write a letter to him.

Tuesday, July 25, 1721

Mama and Papa had a terrible disagreement. Mama spoke so coldly. "You will kill me, William, with your whims," she said. She said other things too about Papa being a "wastrel." I did not want to listen although I think she wanted me to hear.

My letter to Uncle Thaddeus is finished. Mostly I did not know what to say. I cannot put about Mama and Papa's disagreement. I cannot put how I have been working.

I DID tell him how Old Lige has looked after me. I also sent my "best regards" to Nanny. I hope Nanny has not been sent away as I know Mistress Tyler was going to be. I had not thought before how, without me to look after, Nanny will have no job. I do miss her SO, SO MUCH.

Wednesday, July 26, 1721

The sack ship is almost ready to sail. I am filled with thoughts of how Papa might change his mind, so this might be my last night here.

The men are most happy, for Aaron told me he heard from Mr. Chivers that our fish "fetched a good price indeed." Someone is playing a fiddle. Someone is even dancing by one of the fires.

Thursday, July 27, 1721

The ship has left. I am not the only one who does not know how to feel about its going.

"It do be giving you a bit of a pang to think of home now, doesn't it?" Katherine told Peg.

I missed writing how — to load the ship — the men had to go into the forest to collect "dinnage," which is small branches which are used to make a lining so that no damp will enter. Also how, before the fish was loaded, the weight was set down in a book that is called a ledger. And how the measure is in quintals. Captain Jones says 1 quintal is equal to 112 pounds.

Dining with Mama and Papa is HORRIBLE. They do not speak to one another. I think tomorrow for dinner I will simply stay upon the land.

Tuesday, August 1, 1721

I am getting to know when the fish on the flakes are dry enough. I feel it in my fingers, as do Katherine and Peg. I even help sometimes with the fish washing. The fish that are dried are like boards.

The work is very long. Especially for me, who still cannot keep up with it always. We are all of us now very tired. Joshua fell asleep under one of the flakes. Katherine had to wake him. I was MOST tempted to tell her not to, so that he might get into trouble, but I did not.

Mama and Papa seem not to notice that I no longer dine with them. And it is so much JOLLIER eating with the men. The last time I saw Mama she did note that I smelled fishy. I knew I should tell her why, but I did not.

Wednesday, August 2, 1721

Red Indians! One of the men said he thought he had seen one of their boats out on the water. Some of the other men teased him and said he was imagining it. Others looked as if they were not so sure.

"Be any of you seeing them ever?" Jim asked.

Jack said he had "once" but it was only in the distance. He said they had "caused him no trouble."

"Lucky for you then," Silas said.

Thursday, August 3, 1721

Yes, yes! There are Red Indians! Old Lige has seen them also. When he came in he went to Captain Jones to inform him of how he and Rowlie and Silas had rounded a headland and the Red Indian boat had been there. He said the Red Indians went off as fast as they could.

Old Lige says they "be God's creatures." We have no need to be afraid of them. Silas says he has heard they be "thieving perishers." He says we should set a guard.

Friday, August 4, 1721

Captain Jones has told me the Red Indians are called "Beothuks." He says there is nothing but trouble whenever they appear. He has not set a guard but he has ordered the men to be watchful.

Thomas has a big red lump upon his neck. He says it is a "boil." Old Lige has made something which is called a bread poultice to draw out the poison, but I am worried. I think the boil must hurt A GREAT DEAL.

Saturday, August 5, 1721

Old Lige's bread poultice is not working. Thomas's boil grows worse. Mr. Yonge has said he will have to "lance" it. The only lance I have ever heard of is a lance that is carried by soldiers. Surely that would be too big.

Another change has happened. The men turn now to squid for bait. Although catching the squid means that they must do extra work. Rowlie showed me how the squid have these tentacles that hang out from them and how they squirt a liquid that is dark. The liquid is called "ink" but I do not think it would be good to write with. Some of it got onto my apron. Rowlie says it will not be easy to get out.

Sunday, August 6, 1721

The lancing is done. It was done with a knife. I did not ask Thomas if it hurt him. I could tell from how white his face was afterwards that it had. Thomas did not cry out. I have not put it before, but I have noticed that many of the men who work at the cutting are missing at least one of their fingers. I would not like Thomas to lose anything AT ALL.

Monday, August 7, 1721

The Red Indians — no, the Beothuks — seem to have gone. Although thinking about them made me nervous, I still wanted to see them to find out if they looked like the ones in Mistress Tyler's book.

I have sores around my wrists from where my clothing rubs me. Lots of other people have them also. I wish they would get better. They hurt.

Mama and Papa are still not speaking to each other. This means that Papa is spending more time upon the land. Here is something that I notice. Whenever Katherine and Peg's husbands see him they look angry. Eamon most of all.

Mama walks now upon the ship as if she owns it. She holds her back so very straight.

Tuesday, August 8, 1721

I have lost one of the hens. Peter says I should look harder because maybe she is hiding somewhere and has "gone broody." Broody means she will be sitting on her eggs and trying to hatch them instead of leaving them for me.

Wednesday, August 9, 1721

The fishing is still heavy. Old Lige tells me this is most surprising because usually by now "there be some abatement." Thomas is most excited because he thinks he will make lots of money. Old Lige has told him to wait and see. Old Lige says that sometimes when the fish "keep plentiful" the price goes down, so no one is much better off.

I said this is not fair.

"Fair's not got much to do wi' it," Silas told me.

But IT ISN'T FAIR. If I had money and I was buying fish then I would pay A LOT.

Thursday, August 10, 1721

The hen I had lost came back. I was very pleased to see her. That is until Thomas told me that Joshua had found her. She had indeed gone "broody" and she had made herself a nest. I asked Thomas what Joshua had done. He did not want to tell me. Then he said that Joshua had shooed her off and broken her eggs and there were baby chicks inside. I went to the nest myself. I found it was true. I spoke to Joshua of his cruelty. I was shaking inside me but I did it. He was not sorry at all.

Friday, August 11, 1721

Joshua has been punished for his wickedness. I did not say anything to anyone. It was all his own fault. I was walking to the stream and he came up behind me. I think he would have tried to trip me, but Mr. Chivers saw him. Mr Chivers grabbed him by the collar and took him to Captain Jones. Captain Jones made him carry extra water.

Thomas says that Joshua is lucky because Captain Jones could easily have taken some of his pay away. He could also have had him flogged. Thomas says he has heard that flogging is done sometimes. He got Rowlie to tell about it happening on another ship. At first Rowlie was reluctant, but Thomas was so eager he went on. Rowlie said the men were forced to watch "that it might be a lesson to them."

He told how "the poor wretch" was tied to a post and struck with a cat-o'-nine tails, which he says is a whip with many ends. He said the man's cries were awful, especially afterwards when salt was rubbed into his wounds to keep them clean.

I tried not to want to hear Joshua screaming. But then later he was with his friends and he was laughing at me. VERY MUCH I would like to see Joshua hit with a stick or something. Even if it was only once.

Saturday, August 12, 1721

Another sack ship has come. I was in a fever when I saw it. I even went to the *Daisy* for dinner because I could not bear not knowing what might occur.

I had a great surprise. Mama acted as if the ship's coming did not matter. She seemed very determined. She told Papa he would not "best her." She told him she would "do her part."

Perhaps I ought to be pleased. But mostly I am too puzzled. It is as if I do not know Mama at all.

There is a mystery to how the ship found us, for apparently Uncle Thaddeus did not send it. Captain Jones says we should take that as a "sign" that there will be others fishing in this region by next year.

Sunday, August 13, 1721

The men have a Sunday dispensation to cut dinnage and load fish because the ship must leave. It is called the *Patricia*. The captain is a very friendly man. He told me how much of the fish will go to the Roman Catholic countries — the papish ones — because the Roman Catholic people have so many more days upon which they are not allowed to eat meat.

I asked Captain Jones if I might look at the ledger

where the weight of the fish is set down. I also asked him if I might try to tally the numbers. It was the longest line of figuring that I have ever seen. I never did find out just how much fish has been shipped. I can only put it was A LOT. Although, of course, I know that anyway. From all the fish that have been caught.

Monday, August 14, 1721

Papa made me sit with him and tell him about the fish drying. He said it would help him with his work. Then he said the words I use are "common" and that he must have "high" ones.

"Would fulsome faggot be better?" I asked him.

He said he would consider it. Then he went off once more to write.

Mama came out to watch as the *Patricia* was departing. She even waved.

Thursday, August 17, 1721

Aaron is sick. He has had two horrible nosebleeds. Old Lige says it is because he has been eating too much of the cod livers. He says the livers are too rich. Mr. Yonge put a cold cloth over Aaron's nose and one over the back of his neck but still the blood kept running. Mr. Yonge said in England he would also have used leeches, but here he can find none.

I thought how I have eaten the cod livers as well. I spoke to Peter about it. He says they are good for me and that is why oil from them can be sold. He says I am wiser than Aaron for I know "something of restraint."

Lately I have been helping Peter often. Mostly he has me stir things. It is hot by the fire, but stirring is easier than flake work. I help to churn butter as well. Sometimes now the men have time to bring in lobsters. I like the lobsters because they are a change.

Friday, August 18, 1721

At last the fish grow less. I thought the men might be worried, but they are not. This evening, for the first time, everyone seemed to be eating all together. And everyone was talking about their families and how they would be seeing them soon.

Silas said his children would come running. Rowlie started teasing Jim about how he will see someone called "Lily" and Jim went very red. Thomas talked about his mother and his sisters and how he will be "most pleased to greet them."

I slipped away for I did not know what to be saying. I went to find Tibbles to cuddle but, as so often, she is about her own business. From the shore I hear singing and fiddling, but I am feeling sad and strange.

Saturday, August 19, 1721

I crept into Mama's cabin, to where she hangs her gowns. I put my face into the fabric. I tried to remember what it is like to wear such things. And I thought how it will be here when everyone else is gone.

Sunday, August 20, 1721

I hope my prayers reached Heaven. I prayed that Papa would change his mind and we would go HOME.

Tuesday, August 22, 1721

The fish come slower still. I asked Katherine and Peg about who they were most eager to be seeing at home. They looked from one to another. I know there is something they are not telling me. I do not like that AT ALL.

Wednesday, August 23, 1721

A great storm has blown in. Captain Jones says it is a "nor-easter." He says it is a clear sign that soon the *Daisy* must be on her way. I cannot write much because the ship is too much rocking. The wind blows very strong indeed.

Friday, August 25, 1721

Why will Thomas not speak to me? Why does he turn away?

I was coming back from collecting eggs. He and Old Lige were by the stream. They were arguing.

"It be not right," Thomas kept saying.

Then he saw me. Then ran off.

Saturday, August 26, 1721

Old Lige tells me to pay Thomas no mind, but I cannot help it. He is with Joshua now always. He looks at me as Joshua does.

Sunday, August 27, 1721

Another big storm is on its way. I can feel it. Still Thomas will not speak to me or come near me. I am VERY, VERY UPSET.

Monday, August 28, 1721

I have found out why Thomas is angry. It is because Old Lige is to stay here with us and not go home with him. Katherine told me.

Knowing does not help me. Indeed, it makes things worse. I suppose Thomas has been pretending — as I have — that what he did not want would not happen.

I was so grateful to Uncle Thaddeus for giving us Old Lige, but now I am so worried. I have liked being with Thomas SO MUCH. Even if he cannot be my sweetheart. What if he will not speak to me again ever?

I made up this plan. I decided I would go to Papa and tell him he must order Old Lige to leave. Then I thought how I could not bear it here without him. I thought how surely we must perish. I could not bring myself to do anything. I just COULD NOT.

Wednesday, August 30, 1721

Thomas grows worse with me each day. Old Lige tells him he must "mind his manners."

I am all muddled up with confusion. Is it not written in the Bible that each man "must have his station?" Does not Uncle Thaddeus have the right to give commands and orders? Is he not the mer-

chant? Should Thomas not be grateful that Old Lige
will have more work?

He has been arguing with Old Lige again. He has
been talking of how Old Lige is an old man and how
he should remember about Thomas's grandmother.

"What if this be the death of ee?" he has asked
him.

I cannot bear to think of that.

Thursday, August 31, 1721

Captain Jones made an announcement. He said
the *Daisy* must "put to sea" before the mid of
September. He said the fishing boats will not go out
tomorrow. It will be all shore work from now on.

Papa was most excited. "The moment approach-
es," he said. I think he wanted to say more, but I
went away because I could not bear to listen. I
thought of how still he does not know how to do
ANYTHING. Nor Mama either. I wish I had the
Robinson Crusoe book. Perhaps if I could see how
Robinson Crusoe managed I could tell Papa about it
and that would be a help.

I work still with the fish saving but I do it with a
heavy heart.

Friday, September 1, 1721

Captain Jones has asked Papa if he does not wish to change his mind. Papa has said ABSOLUTELY he does not.

Captain Jones sighed as I remember Uncle Thaddeus doing. He told me we will have his tilt because it is the biggest and it has the best "bits of furniture." Also because it may be warmer because it is lined more securely inside and out. And because there are boards upon the floor. Captain Jones says he will have the men mound earth and sods around the bottom. That will be for extra warmth still.

Saturday, September 2, 1721

It is horrible to be so sad when everyone else is so happy. Only Katherine and Peg and Eamon and Aengus are different. They act as if they are preparing instead of going away.

The men cheered as the first of the dinnage was loaded. Some of them are taking the stages and flakes down. This is for wood for cooking on the way home and for wood for us to have here. The tilts that are not needed will be taken apart as well.

Sunday, September 3, 1721

Reverend Jacobs gave thanks for a good season and for the successful discovery of this new fishing place. I tried to be filled up with thankfulness but it is hard. After the service Papa kept rubbing his hands together. He went around exclaiming about how soon this would be "his kingdom, his domain."

Monday, September 4, 1721

I have been to Papa and asked him to relent.

"But this is only the beginning," he told me.

For a moment I thought of somehow taking away his papers and his quills and ink and destroying them. But then I could not think of how to do it. And anyway I did not think that it would work.

Instead I went to Captain Jones's tilt and put some purple daisy flowers upon the table. Mama says she will "visit the place" tomorrow. I cannot imagine what she will say when she does so. I cannot imagine how we will all of us live together there. Or perhaps I can and that is worse.

Tuesday, September 5, 1721

I am filled with AMAZEMENT. Mama left the ship in her most stately way. She walked as if she were a queen. She stepped inside Captain Jones's tilt as if there were nothing the matter.

She said the place would "do" for her. But then she said that we could not all of us live together in it. Papa looked most nervous. Mama took little notice of him.

"There must be a place for dining and a place for the others to be sleeping," she decreed.

Captain Jones said he would arrange it. Mama went back to the ship. Captain Jones suggested to Papa that he might take the tilt that had belonged to Mr. Chivers. Papa agreed to this. Then both of them looked at me. For a moment, I did not know what to do. I wanted to say I would stay with Old Lige, but I knew that would not be proper. The words just came out of me.

"I will have my own tilt also," I said.

At once I thought I should not have done that, but already Papa was looking most relieved. He told me I might choose "whatever might seem best for me."

I have chosen the tilt that is next to Old Lige's, although I suspect Mama would not wish me to have done so. It is where Jack and his crew have been living. There will be more room than in my cabin here. I think, however, that Captain Jones is worried. I heard him talking to Old Lige about all the extra fires to be required "when winter falls." He says from all he has heard, the winter is a bitter time.

Wednesday, September 6, 1721

Some of the men must now put more rinds on the other tilts we will use also. They must mound up the earth as they have begun to do around the tilt that will be Mama's. It will take many days.

I went to Thomas specially. I told him I was sorry for all of this. I told him it is not my fault. He shifted from foot to foot but he would not answer me.

Old Lige said again I should not worry. He said that Uncle Thaddeus is paying him well "for his trouble." He also said, "This be the way of the world, my maid."

Even though I am sad, I liked him calling me "my maid." He has not done so before. He has always called me "Mistress" or "Little Mistress" or "Mistress Sophie" just like everyone else.

Thursday, September 7, 1721

Truly, truly, God MUST work "in a mysterious way." What I prayed for will not happen. But I will have THE NEXT BEST THING!!!

Finally, I have found out why Katherine and Peg

and Eamon and Aengus have been acting so strangely. THEY ARE STAYING HERE. They have "negotiated" with Captain Jones that the money they have earned will come to them in "supplies." I do not know when they did this. I just know it has been done. Papa is raging but Captain Jones will not "undo it." I want to dance and shout.

Friday, September 8, 1721

Papa has decreed that if Katherine and Peg and Eamon and Aengus are to live here they must move their tilts across the stream. Eamon and Aengus are VERY ANGRY but they are doing it. I think that Katherine and Peg are angry also. But they are not angry with me. Mostly now that it is all out in the open they are pleased and excited. Peg even says that maybe across the stream will be better for them, for then "they will have land that is really, really all their own."

Saturday, September 9, 1721

The *Daisy* has been re-rigged. Her masts stand tall again. Peter says that on Monday there will be a great slaughtering. The pigs and the calf (which is not a calf any longer) will be killed. He says it "be early in the year" to do such things, but that

Captain Jones has decreed it for he wishes the meat to be salted and shared out before the *Daisy* departs. He wishes to do all he can to ensure our "proper provisioning all winter long."

Peter is shaking his head about the cow. He does not believe we will be able to keep her. He says again that the hay Uncle Thaddeus sent with us "be not enough." He says he is sure Uncle Thaddeus must have thought that we would be able to cut more during the summer but there has been "no hope for that." Still, he says we should have milk as long as we can.

P.S. How could I have forgotten to put that the cow's name is Bessie? And that I am VERY GLAD the chickens will remain?

Sunday, September 10, 1721

I prayed with THANKFULNESS. There was Holy Communion for the ship's departure. As I watched the men being given the bread and wine for Jesus' blood and body, I thought how it is not long now until I too shall be able to take part in this.

Monday, September 11, 1721

Peter told me I should stay upon the ship for the slaughtering and so I did that, although I did look out. There was much noise and squealing and the boys were so excited that they ran about. ESPECIALLY JOSHUA, of course. When the animals were dead they were hung on wooden tripods so the blood could drip from them. Peter says the blood is good for sausage. The slaughtering seems another lot of trouble for the men to be going to when they must want to be thinking only of setting out. And it is ALL on our behalf. The meat is not the only food we will have. Fish will be left for us also. As well as peas and flour and other supplies. And hay for Bessie, of course.

Tuesday, September 12, 1721

The fishing boats have been returned to the *Daisy* and readied for the voyage. Only Old Lige's boat is left because Captain Jones says that it may be of use.

The *Daisy* seems so noisy with all the men once more on board.

Wednesday, September 13, 1721

Papa has decreed that when the ship leaves we are not to speak to Katherine and Peg and Eamon and Aengus. It is crucial to his scheme that we should seem to be alone. Again, I want to beg and plead with him. AS LOUDLY AS I CAN.

How can I not speak to them? When I have been with them all summer? When I like them SO, SO MUCH?

Thursday, September 14, 1721

Katherine and Peg and Eamon and Aengus have heard of Papa's decree. Eamon is even angrier than before.

Friday, September 15, 1721

I am in my own tilt. My trunk has been brought to me. Already I have set Eliza on my bed. Tibbles is here. I am hoping she is going to stay with me. I know I will be happier if she does, although I would not try to stop her going on the ship. I have picked flowers for myself and I have made a place for my writing things on the table that once belonged to Mr. Yonge. Tonight I will sleep on the ship for the last time.

Saturday, September 16, 1721

How sad, sad, SAD I am. I have said goodbye to everyone. Except Joshua and Thomas. Thomas would not speak to me. He said goodbye only to Old Lige.

My mattress has been brought from my cabin. Reverend Jacobs's bed has been removed here also. Jack and his crew slept on the ground on spruce boughs. As did most of the men. Captain Jones did not think this would be right for me. I could not disagree.

Sunday, September 17, 1721

The *Daisy* has gone. She went "on the tide." I wanted to climb up on the clifftop to see her with her sails set, but Papa is so fixed on how I must not cross the stream. Old Lige went over. He picked berries — the red ones that are called partridge berries and the ones that are called blueberries also. He brought them back to cheer me up. I was not very cheered for I found myself burning with anger inside me. So what if Papa wishes to make money and become famous? SO WHAT? SO WHAT?

I went to the stream purposely when I could see that Katherine and Peg were there. Katherine just turned away. I saw that Eamon was watching.

Anger was coming from him also.

Peg said, "Mistress Sophie, you must leave us now in peace."

I turned away as she had requested me, but my heart was breaking.

I hate it with the places where the flakes and the stages and the stage heads stood, all empty now. I hate it with the other tilts gone and everything all BARE.

Tuesday, September 19, 1721

I was right to know that without Old Lige we could not manage. I would be so lonely if he was not here. All day I have been with him. That is one good thing that can happen.

We sat in his tilt — the cooking tilt. Tibbles was with us. We talked A LOT, for the rain was falling and the wind was blowing. I could tell he was worried for Thomas. When the tilt shook with the storm's violence he frowned and said, "Perhaps it be not so bad far out."

He is also worried about the meals he must be making. He says he has never cooked "for any fine folks before." I told him I thought his food was delicious. It is indeed much like Peter's, for he must use the same ingredients. We cannot eat the salted meat yet. It is too soon.

Why do I remember to put some things and not others? Why have I not written that Papa's beard is not the only thing that has grown upon him? His hair has grown also and long ago he gave up wearing his wig. I thought about all this as I was sitting with him and Mama at dinner. Mama now insists again upon this. She seems to have forgotten how little I was dining with them before the *Daisy* left. Luckily she does not insist on my taking my midday meal also with her and Papa.

Thursday, September 21, 1721

A blue sunny day. Old Lige is teaching me to milk Bessie. I did not get any milk but he says that "be usual." She must get used to the feel of my hands. Bessie feeds now in the places where the trees were. Some greenery grows there again.

Papa has decided he must be the one who will make the larger table Mama has insisted upon for the dining tilt. I do not understand why he will not ask Old Lige to show him how to do it. Why he keeps saying he must "learn the rough of the wood" himself. If making the table is so important to him, why did he not seek to learn of such things before?

Saturday, September 23, 1721

Eamon and Aengus took the boat and went fishing. Old Lige says the boat was left for all of us and must be shared. He says too the fish will no longer "be in numbers" but there will be enough for ourselves "for some good while."

Katherine and Peg continue gathering seaweed. They are putting it upon the land. The seaweed is for making the soil good. Old Lige says they hope to have a farm.

Aengus has this little tin whistle. He plays it sometimes in the evenings. Today Old Lige and I stood by the door together to listen. Old Lige tapped his feet with the fast tunes but I liked the slow ones best.

Sunday, September 24, 1721

I am writing THE MOST EXTRAORDINARY THING that I have written. Beothuk people came this morning. I was all by myself when I saw them. It was early. I had gone outside because I heard voices and I thought it might be Katherine and Peg.

I knew who the Beothuks were because they had red smeared on them and they were dressed in skins. I was so surprised I just stood there. Then I noticed that off by herself there was a girl. It was as if we were drawn to each other on strings. I had Eliza in my hands still from the nighttime. I do not know what possessed me, but I held Eliza out as if she were a gift.

I would have tried to talk to the girl but her people grabbed her. Papa and Old Lige had come out by that time. Papa grabbed me. The Beothuks ran to their boats and began to leave. But the girl did not drop Eliza. She held her tight.

Eamon and Aengus came then also. They started shouting. But it was too late. The Beothuk people were gone. Papa said I had been "most brave." I do not know why, but I think there was not anything to be brave about.

Papa has taken out the gun he brought to hunt with. He has ordered Old Lige to clean it for him. When Mama heard what had happened she told him to see to it that we are not "slaughtered in our beds." I tried to say that the Beothuks could have "slaughtered" us already, for there were far more of them than there are of us. Mama would not listen. Papa would not either. They NEVER LISTEN to me.

P.S. The Beothuks did look a little like the Red Indians Mistress Tyler showed me, but they were not terrifying AT ALL.

Monday, September 25, 1721

Papa walks with his gun along the shore. Eamon and Aengus take turns upon the clifftop. I think that they are keeping watch. Only Old Lige and I seem to consider the Beothuks may have come here for some other reason than to harm us.

Old Lige believes they did not expect to see anyone. He believes they were looking for things that had been left behind. He reckons "a nail may be turned to a good few purposes." He is also much admiring of "how fair their boats go through the water." I should have put about them — that they are not rowed but paddled and they are long and thin with a high bit in the middle and at both ends.

Wednesday, September 27, 1721

The Beothuk people have not come back. Mama seems much relieved. I wonder about the girl. I wonder about Eliza. Will her people let the girl keep her? Why was the girl so interested in me?

Papa has forgotten about the table so Old Lige is making it after all. I am getting better at milking Bessie. I filled HALF THE BUCKET today.

Old Lige says that before the winter comes we must have the wood that was not taken onto the *Daisy* cut into logs and stacked up. He saws and, some, I carry. I do not think I could have lifted one log when I came here and now I can move lots. Old Lige is also building a place so Bessie will have shelter. It is like all the other buildings — out of logs. I think he likes building things. He says he is going to make himself a bed, for his bones "be too old to sleep on spruce boughs all the winter long."

Sunday, October 1, 1721

Old Lige told Papa that Eamon and Aengus must be allowed to come and get wood also, "else in the winter they will freeze." Papa said they should cut down trees.

"But trees be green," Old Lige said. "They be not firewood for another season."

I did not think Old Lige could be so insistent, but he was. In the end Papa agreed, as long as Eamon and Aengus "are not spoken to." I do not want to speak to Eamon. But I do want to speak to Katherine and to Peg.

I have found out a secret. Old Lige puts milk by the stream in a bucket each day and Katherine and Peg come to fetch it. Old Lige does not know I know this. Does he think that I would tell?

How strange that on Sundays we can have no services. It means that each day is like unto the next. It is lucky Captain Jones made me a present of a little calendar. If he had not, I think I might lose account of things and not know which day was which.

Ducks came into the cove this morning. Papa saw them. He was most excited. He talked of the shooting parties at Deer Park. The ducks flew on but he has said that tomorrow Old Lige must row him out at dawning to a place he has seen that is hidden, where he will wait. Shooting is "gentlemen's work."

Monday, October 2, 1721

Papa did not shoot one duck only. He shot two. Old Lige plucked off the feathers. Mama said the meat tasted "too wild." Papa said that "supplementing our meagre fare" is something he must do.

Tuesday, October 3, 1721

Mama has started more painting. She says painting is "the only occupation fit for a lady here."

We are making piles of wood by each tilt. Even though I am stronger the work is VERY heavy. Old Lige works calmly and steadily. I try to be like him but sometimes I get into a flurry. I cannot seem to help myself.

Bessie gave me all the milk she had today. I was so grateful I kissed her on the nose. I also asked Old

Lige if I could take the milk to the stream for Katherine and Peg. He smiled at me and told me that I could. He gave me some eggs to take as well.

The hens are laying less now. Old Lige says we may have to kill some of them because in the winter they will not be able to peck in the earth. They will have only scraps from our table and it will not be enough. I wanted to cry out against this, but I see that there are some things that before I have not had to know about, which now I must.

Friday, October 6, 1721

Mama was very disturbed. It had to do with her painting — which was of the sea. Papa and I went from her after dinner early. I was glad, for it gave me longer to sit with Old Lige. His tilt is cozy from the cooking fire. Mine remains QUITE COLD. He made me some hot milk to drink before bedtime and he poured milk into a dish for Tibbles as well.

I am learning about fire tending. Old Lige is very patient. He was not even angry when I made too much blazing so that the pot boiled up too high. I am sorry he has to bend so much. I mentioned this to him. He said what he has said before to me. About it being "the way of the world."

Sunday, October 8, 1721

Papa tried to light the fire in Mama's tilt but he created only smoke. I was very pleased with myself for I was able to set the matter to rights. I think I could teach Papa also, but he will not learn.

I am not going to write for long because I realize I have been neglecting my Bible. To show how sorry I am, I am going to start at the beginning and read a chapter every day until I get to the end. This will not be easy in the light from the candle but I am going to try.

Monday, October 9, 1721

Papa shot a goose. It is such a relief to know that there is something he is good at. And he is so very pleased. I helped Old Lige with the plucking. I was going to throw the feathers away but he said I should use them for a pillow. And he gave me a little cloth bag to make the pillow with. I asked him if he misses Aaron and Rowlie and Silas and the others. He sat down and he sighed.

I did not put before how, after a while, I really was not wearing my shoes very often. I have to now all the time because it is colder. This is a pity because they pinch A LOT.

Mama commanded me to bring her some beach

stones. She put them by two plates upon the table. She said she is painting what is called a "still life."

Wednesday, October 11, 1721

I heard Eamon shouting at Katherine. I did not like it. Although later I did not mind so much when Katherine started shouting back.

I asked Old Lige if he would take me out upon the sea when he went fishing. I liked being there in his boat A LOT. It was a very fine day. We admired how now there are some leaves back in the forest that are different colours.

"Ee art like another grandchild to me almost," he said as we were coming in.

Then he begged my pardon.

I am sure it is wrong of me, but my heart leaped up when I heard him. I know it is not fitting but I would like to be like Old Lige's grandchild A GREAT DEAL.

Friday, October 13, 1721

Friday the Thirteenth is supposed to be an un-lucky day but on this one nothing unlucky hap-pened at all. Indeed, I learned how to heat a rock and put it in my bed to warm it. I did this also for

Mama and Papa. Tibbles is sitting on top of the covers where my rock is even now.

Old Lige and I are trying to cut some of the greenery Bessie does not eat and bring it here for the winter to add to Uncle Thaddeus's hay. Old Lige shakes his head and says "there be so little," but to me it seems we have created quite a pile.

A whole chapter of the Bible is too hard. I will read only half a one. The last one was all about how long everybody like Jared and Noah and Methuselah lived. It was hundreds of years. I have never known anyone who was even one hundred. I wonder if I ever shall.

Sunday, October 15, 1721

Old Lige says Peg is going to have a baby. He says if we were home he would not mention such a thing to me but since there is no one else to tell me, he sees "no harm."

I do not know whether to be sad or excited. What if the baby comes and I am not allowed to see it? I prayed A LONG TIME that God might help Papa and Eamon to change their minds.

A strong wind is blowing again. Leaves are whirling. Branches of trees are dancing. The waves of the sea wash high. Does that not sound a little like Papa's poetry? Is it not different from how I have written before?

Tuesday, October 17, 1721

The wind continues. Again Mama seems upset. Again I think it has to do with her painting. Mama is not like Papa. She casts away much of what she has done. I chanced to pick up a paper she had thrown down. (No, I did not. I picked it up deliberately. I hid it in my apron because I wanted to see.) The stones and the plate were there but everything in the picture seemed to be all moving — like waves.

Old Lige is teaching me to whittle. He says it will be something for the long winter evenings. Whittling means taking a piece of wood and carving it into whatever shape you like. I made a little boat like the boats of the Beothuk people. Old Lige said I might try it in the stream and so I did that. It floated VERY WELL.

More and more I am helping him with the cooking. He has shown me how to wash the salt from the pork and how to soak the little dried peas we have so often and the biscuit too. Also how to make sure there is always spruce beer.

I told him I was reading the Bible and he asked me to read it to him. I started again at the beginning of Genesis, Chapter 8. It is about Noah and the flood. I have never thought what it would be like not to be able to read before. Perhaps I should have. Old Lige said my reading to him was as good as "being in church."

Saturday, October 21, 1721

I realize that tomorrow is my birthday and I shall be thirteen years old. How strange that I have not thought of it. Last year Uncle Thaddeus brought me gowns. This year what I really need are some new aprons and new footwear. Thank goodness my cloak still fits me. Today I wore it inside even. Mama was wearing her cloak also, though it is much more fine.

Sunday, October 22, 1721

It was as I expected. My birthday passed without Papa and Mama noticing. I was a little disappointed but not much. After all, I had only barely remembered it myself. Perhaps birthdays are really only for children.

I keep thinking about Peg. I think too about Mama's sickness on the ship. I do not want Peg to get sick with the same thing. I watch her often when I am outside and she is also. I think perhaps she would not like it but I cannot help myself.

I remember how she and Katherine would speak of when they would have children. And of how Peg would say that she knew it would not please Aengus, but what she really wanted was a little daughter to have first.

I wish I knew truly how babies happen. Old Lige and I have been reading about how, after the flood, God told people to go forth and "be fruitful and multiply." This must have something to do with it. But what?

Thursday, October 26, 1721

Papa was walking on the shore and I saw smoke coming from his pocket. I ran to tell him about it. At first he tried to stop me disturbing him "when the muse was with him," but it was lucky that I did. He had put his pipe into his pocket by mistake.

I think I have not said that Mama continues to walk out as she did on the *Daisy*. Sometimes she has me walk with her. Sometimes she even has me point things out to her. Like the little sea pigeons that are still here. Or the line where the seaweed comes.

Saturday, October 28, 1721

Katherine and Peg and Eamon and Aengus are still bringing seaweed. Old Lige says he would like to give them the droppings from Bessie and the chickens. I suspect he may find a way to do this.

Today is MUCH, MUCH COLDER. There was a skiff of ice around the edges of the stream. I was very glad to put my head up against Bessie, who is so warm always. Mama complained about the cold a GREAT, GREAT deal.

Sunday, October 29, 1721

I asked Old Lige how always and always he knows when it is Sunday. He says he takes sticks and makes marks. There is a mark for each day until he gets to seven and that "be all he needs."

I am getting on with my whittling although I am doing something harder. I am trying to make a little doll to take Eliza's place.

Tuesday, October 31, 1721

How nervous I am about blowing out my candle for it is All Hallows Eve — the day when Nanny would tell me "ghoulie things might be about." I asked Uncle Thaddeus about this once. He said it was all nonsense. But Nanny was so certain and even Old Lige said I should be careful, so I am not sure.

Wednesday, November 1, 1721

All Saints' Day. If I could choose a saint then I would choose Old Lige. At dinner Mama spoke sharply to him because she said the stew was "unacceptable." I wanted to turn her plate over so she would have nothing. Old Lige simply nodded and said he would serve something better on another time.

I do know saints are supposed to have been martyred and done miracles (or kill dragons like St. George, of course) but Old Lige is a MIRACLE to me.

P.S. I should record that nothing untoward happened on All Hallows. I took some while getting to sleep because I was listening for noises. Then I slept safe and sound.

Thursday, November 2, 1721

Papa cut his hand. He did it sharpening his quill. He made a great fuss about it. Old Lige bandaged it up for him. He also put salt upon it so that it would not become infected. The salt made me think of what Rowlie told me — about what happens when a man is flogged. Afterwards Papa could do nothing for the rest of the day.

I did A LOT because Old Lige killed two of the chickens and, of course, they had to be plucked and also cooked. The smell of the cooking was lovely. I had been so sorry about the chickens and then I was not sorry any longer. I wanted Mama to say something nice to Old Lige about the meal but she did not, so after it was over and we were back in Old Lige's tilt again, I did.

Friday, November 3, 1721

I am worried. I was helping Old Lige bring wood to put outside Mama's tilt. His breath would not come to him. He had to sit down. Even later, when he was breathing properly once more, he let me do things he does not normally. I am afraid he may be ill.

Saturday, November 4, 1721

The rain has turned to freezing. There is ice on everything. It pounds against the roof. Mama and Papa had to eat each in their own places. Old Lige slipped and fell when he was bringing their food to them. Afterwards he was limping. He said his hip was sore.

Sunday, November 5, 1721

At home it would be Guy Fawkes Day with bonfires. I wish we were all there for it. Old Lige has pains in his chest. He keeps bending over, coughing.

I am going to stop now and pray for him. Then I will read the next chapter in my Bible. Perhaps God will see that I am trying and He will look down and help.

Monday, November 6, 1721

Old Lige stayed abed. All he could manage was to remind me of the things that must be done. I wanted to tell Mama and Papa but he would not let me. I did my best with the meals and with keeping the fires going and with the milking and feeding the chickens but it was VERY HARD.

Tuesday, November 7, 1721

Tomorrow, if Old Lige is not better, I am going to go to Katherine and Peg. I HAVE TO! I HAVE TO! In case they know some medicine which would help.

At least the ice is gone. That is better, of course. Still now it is so cold AGAIN.

I have been delaying lighting a fire in my own tilt to avoid the extra work of it. Now I have no time.

Wednesday, November 8, 1721

Old Lige has died. I went to him this morning. I thought he was still sleeping but he was not. I ran, without thinking, for Katherine and Peg, because I did not know what should be done with his body. They came weeping, saying what a good, good man he was. All day, they have sat with me beside him. Although Katherine cooked also for Mama and Papa.

Thursday, November 9, 1721

Eamon and Aengus dug a grave for Old Lige. It is where the crosses are. Papa read the service for him in a very deep voice. It was horrible seeing his body put into the ground, even if he was wrapped in a blanket. It was worse when the earth was shovelled over him. I had to make myself stand there watching, but then when it was all over I did not want to leave.

Why did I not go to Katherine and Peg right when I knew he was ill? I want to write and write about Old Lige. My heart is too heavy. No words will come.

Friday, November 10, 1721

Papa says Old Lige's heart gave out. I do not know what that means. Mama says nothing — NOTHING AT ALL.

Saturday, November 11, 1721

Aengus has put a cross on Old Lige's grave. I went to sit beside it. I miss him so much and yet I cannot cry for him. The tears feel as if they are a stone kept hard within my chest.

Sunday, November 12, 1721

Papa says he is counting on me for I will know "our daily tasks." I suppose this is true. But I think there is too much for one person to be doing.

I have been trying to pray but I am angry with God that He has taken Old Lige from us. Even if I know we are supposed to believe that everything God does is good for us and according to HIS PLAN.

Monday, November 13, 1721

Papa says he is making a poem "for our dead hero." What is a poem compared with Old Lige himself — ALIVE? Even Tibbles seems to be looking for him. She stands in the doorway of the cooking tilt and meows.

Tuesday, November 14, 1721

I did not put it before but now I cannot help myself. Each day I am more certain that Old Lige would be still living if he had not stayed here. Each day I know more clearly that he died for Mama and for Papa and FOR ME.

I do not know what to do for the guilt of it. I am glad that Katherine and Peg and Eamon and Aengus have gone back to their own side of the stream again, for I do not want them to see me and think about that too.

Poor, poor Old Lige's wife who does not even know of this.

And poor, poor Thomas. Was he not right to be angry with me? Was I not wrong to be upset at him?

Wednesday, November 15, 1721

There is TOO MUCH to do. Papa tries to help but he does not stay with anything. When he went to get water he spilled it — as I did in the beginning. The difference is that Papa said he would not fetch water any more. The worst is the fires. I cannot keep them burning — except for the cooking fire. Mama and Papa complain CONSTANTLY because they are both cold.

I want to remind them that at Deer Park it was cold also. That we had to be huddling by the fires there often too. At least here — in the tilts — there is less space to be heating.

Mostly I want to tell them that the cold is NOT MY FAULT.

Bessie was bawling. Katherine came quietly. She milked her in my stead. She says Bessie will grow sick if the milking is "not regular."

Papa did not seem to mind when Katherine and Peg and Eamon and Aengus came for Old Lige's funeral but I fear he will mind if he sees them now.

Saturday, November 18, 1721

I cannot keep up. I cannot. I cannot hurry enough.

Sunday, November 19, 1721

Mama has rescued us. She has made "an arrangement." To do it she bid me take her across the stream. Everyone there was most amazed to see her.

"I have come on a business matter," she told them.

The "matter" is that Katherine will work for us and do what Old Lige did. Eamon wanted to know what Katherine would be paid "for her trouble." Mama decreed that Papa would "arrange it." She came back and stayed closeted with him a long time. He did not look pleased but he crossed the stream himself then. He returned saying he "had parted with a few trifles." I have not found out what they are. Mostly, I do not care. I am just SO PLEASED that once more I will be seeing Katherine (and perhaps Peg also) EVERY SINGLE DAY.

Monday, November 20, 1721

When Katherine got here she stood in the doorway to the cooking tilt and smiled a great, big SMILE. I know partly she is glad because she got what she thinks is "a fair, good bargain." The bargain is the chickens and Bessie. Or the new cow and chickens that Captain Jones will bring to supply the men if Bessie and the chickens "last not the winter out."

She talked MUCH about the farm she and Eamon and Peg and Aengus will have. She explained how most of the money they had earned was spent already. Not just for the provisioning for this winter but because they have arranged that, when the *Daisy* returns, Captain Jones will bring them a walking plough and two more pigs, as well as other things that they will need.

I believe also that she smiled because she was glad to be with me. She said all the keeping apart was "a lot of old nonsense." Perhaps then it is true about God. Perhaps — although I would not have him dead FOR ANYTHING — there is something useful that has come to us from Old Lige's death.

The chickens and Bessie will stay where they are. Katherine says moving their houses is too much trouble. The eggs and the milk will be shared still. Only now there will be no secrets. And Katherine and Peg and Eamon and Aengus will be giving these things to us instead of the other way round.

I am glad Tibbles did not get to be part of any bargain. Probably no one else would have thought that she might.

Tuesday, November 21, 1721

Mama has gone back to painting. Papa has gone back to writing. For them, nothing is different. For me, once more, everything is changed. Peg came over today. She talked to me about the baby. We sat together A LONG TIME.

Katherine says from now on whatever must be done will be done between us. She will get Eamon and Aengus to finish the wood cutting and stacking and they will go to try to find Bessie more food.

Wednesday, November 22, 1721

When I went to the cooking tilt I saw that Katherine was putting some of Old Lige's ladles and spoons in different places and that she had piled some cloths upon his bed. The tears came welling in my eyes. Katherine put her arms around me.

I cried a LONG, LONG TIME. I told her how I am certain Mama and Papa and I have killed him almost. She did not argue with me.

There is a way where the crying has made me feel better. Still it hurts and hurts inside me — knowing that I can cry and cry forever. Old Lige will never return.

And I will never be free of knowing that perhaps I was part of sending him to his death.

Thursday, November 23, 1721

Papa says he has "seen his mistake." He knows now it was not right for us to be trying to be here all by ourselves. He told Mama and me how in *Robinson Crusoe* there is someone called Friday and how he should have remembered that. At dinner he thanked Mama for her "inspired act."

He talked on and on about how it is "only proper" that "the Irish should serve us." I cannot believe that this is so. And yet again I know that if I were still at Deer Park I would never ever have thought that I should disagree. I do so hope that Katherine did not hear him. Although perhaps those who must be servants grow accustomed to such things.

I should put that Katherine does not stay all the time as Old Lige did. She goes home after dinner when all the work is done. By then the cooking tilt is so warm that from now on I am going to stay there. I think that Old Lige would be pleased about that. I think he would say it is "sensible." Keeping one less tilt heated will make things easier and that will be good.

Friday, November 24, 1721

Something happened to me that has not ever before. I laughed until the tears ran down my face. It was Katherine and Peg's fault for they started remembering a man from their village who kept sneezing in church one time. They acted it out between them. They laughed and then I did also. Until my sides ached. What would Mama say if she knew? We even disturbed Tibbles. She stuck her tail in the air and stalked away.

Saturday, November 25, 1721

Eamon and Aengus do not know that I can now understand much Gaelic or that I hear them when they are grumbling (and laughing even sometimes) at Mama and Papa as they work with the wood. I try not to listen but I cannot seem to help it. Part of me wants to tell them to stop it. Indeed I know I should do this. But there is another part of me that often agrees with what they say.

Katherine is teaching me to darn my stockings. This is a good thing for they have many holes. Darning is not so very different from embroidery so I am learning quite fast. Katherine says she will help me with where my aprons are torn next, although she will not be able to do anything about how much I have grown. This is getting to be more and more of a problem. When I put about my birthday I should have put that I need new bedgowns and new petticoats for they have also become too small.

Katherine is worried about clothes altogether. She says she had not thought it possible that there would be no sheep here and so no wool for her and Peg to spin and weave. She is troubled especially because already it is so cold. She thinks as time goes by they will need more clothes than ever.

She says she hopes Captain Jones will remember he agreed to bring new clothes for them in the springtime. But how can she and the others go on always buying? And how would they have sheep anyway? Is it not hard enough to feed the one poor cow?

Here is a secret. I have done something bad but it was for a good reason. When Katherine was telling me about the clothes she said how Peg does not know what to do about garments for the baby that is coming. When Mama was out walking I went into her tilt. I took one of her gowns from her trunk. It was at the bottom. I do not think she will miss it. I gave it to Katherine to carry over the stream so Peg can have it. There is much, much fabric in it.

Katherine did not just thank me. She laughed.

Wednesday, November 29, 1721

It has snowed. As Peg was coming over to visit, Aengus threw a snowball at her. She turned and threw one back. How different they are from Mama and Papa. Could I be like them if I were to have a husband? I think I would prefer to be.

Later Katherine and Peg fell to talking of how at home in the evenings the people near where they lived would gather together to sing and dance. Katherine said she is "fine and glad" that Aengus has his little tin whistle but "it do not be making enough of a din."

Katherine said how she misses her father and her mother and Peg said that as well. It made me miss Deer Park and Uncle Thaddeus. And Nanny too, of course.

Friday, December 1, 1721

Another new month. I went to Old Lige's grave. I told him that it is less time now until Thomas will be coming to see him. Then I thought about Thomas and all the others arriving and finding what had happened and I was afraid.

The snow only stayed a few days. But in that time I was able to see how much Bessie has eaten of what we gathered. I understand then more of what Peter and Old Lige were always saying about the not-enough hay.

Mama spoke at dinner of how life here is "tedious." Papa asked her if she would have him read to her from what he has been writing but she said no. It made me think of my Bible and how I had been reading to Old Lige. I have not been able to go on since he went from us. Each time I try, a lump comes to my throat.

Sunday, December 3, 1721

Here is something most surprising. Mama came to the cooking tilt. She asked Katherine if we had all that we are needing. She has never done such a thing before. For a moment I thought that she might sit down and stay but then she did not do so. Can it be that she is lonely? Or that she is curious about when we are talking and she cannot hear?

Monday, December 4, 1721

Here is something else surprising. Often when Katherine is busy she sings. I know some of the songs, of course, so now I join in. This evening after dinner I thought I heard Papa humming one of the tunes.

The wood is all stacked so Eamon and Aengus no longer come here much. Katherine says men often "have it good" in the winter for there is less outside work for them whereas the women's work — the work of the household — must always go on. Although perhaps there will be work for the men in adding more rinds to the tilts if the weather "grow truly cold." The wind is rising and the temperature is falling. I know that there will be a storm.

Wednesday, December 6, 1721

The storm did come. It brought more snow but it blew through quickly. Eamon and Aengus went hunting for rabbits. They did not catch any. Katherine says they have no need of a gun such as Papa has, for they hunt "the poor man's way" — with snares.

I do not expect it is polite to write this but Peg's

stomach is sticking out in front of her now a long way. She has told me that is where the baby is and she has let me feel it kicking. At least, when it comes to babies being born, I now know something. Even if I still have not found out how it is they get in and out.

Saturday, December 9, 1721

Eamon and Aengus caught rabbits — which Katherine says actually are more like what she would have called hares. The fur is almost white. Katherine says she thinks that is for the winter. She took the skins off very carefully. She says there is "nothing like a rabbit skin" for keeping a young one warm.

Aengus smiled at me! He had come into the cooking tilt to fetch Peg and she dropped her mitten and I picked it up for her because now it is so hard for her to bend. Aengus seemed VERY PLEASED. I think he loves Peg a great deal.

Later I came upon the doll I was making to replace Eliza. I started working on it once more so that I may give it to Peg's baby when the time shall come.

I have found out I like rabbit meat and so does Tibbles. A LOT.

Sunday, December 10, 1721

Peg brought the garments she has made for the baby out of the gown I gave her from Mama's trunk. There are gowns and caps and petticoats. Peg fears she has made them too large because she does not know where other clothes will come from, but they seem most small to me. Peg is VERY EXCITED about the baby coming. She says she thinks that it will be in about two weeks. I told her it would be in time for Christmas. That is when I found out that neither she nor Katherine nor Eamon nor Aengus know what date it is. I promised that I would inform them. And then I thought again about how it is not to be able to read.

Monday, December 11, 1721

One of Katherine's eyes is black and swollen. I heard her saying to Peg that Eamon had hit her. I cannot believe how such a thing could be. All day I tried to help her but it was as if she were angry with me as well. She made much noise with the cooking. She pushed past me when the beans were needed from the barrel instead of asking me to fetch them for her. She hardly spoke to me at all.

Tuesday, December 12, 1721

Katherine was more herself today but her eye is still black. I wish Eamon was not her husband. I wish she had someone like Aengus.

I look at him and Peg and think how it would be good to be married, but then I look at Katherine and Eamon — and Mama and Papa even — and think that it would not.

I have given up on the Old Testament. Christmas is coming so I am going to read about that.

Thursday, December 14, 1721

Papa has made a GRAND ANNOUNCEMENT. He has said that tomorrow after dinner he will "deliver" some of his writing for the benefit of Mama and of me. He seems to have forgotten that Mama said she did not wish to hear it. I am afraid to listen. In case I do not like what he has said.

I have been tempted to ask him about the poem he promised for Old Lige but, each time, when the chance has arisen, I have let the words go from me. This is because I do not believe Papa would under-stand Old Lige well enough to describe him as he truly was.

I notice that Katherine stays longer in the evenings. She says nothing of this but I suspect she is hoping that Eamon will be sleeping before she comes home. I think if Captain Jones was here still he would put a stop to Eamon's behaviour. I wish there were someone else who could do so in his stead.

Friday, December 15, 1721

Papa began with our leaving. His writing is indeed very "poetical." He talked of "crowds of well-wishers, admiring of our adventure," when I remember only Uncle Thaddeus being there. Many, many pages were passed and we were only on the third day of the voyage. Here there was much about the "rigours." I think that must have had to do with when we were all so sick.

When Papa was finished for the night he put down his papers as if Mama and I were supposed to applaud him. For a moment Mama did nothing so I started clapping. She did then join in.

P.S. Captain Jones was right when he said the winter would be "bitter." By the time we left the dining tilt I was shivering. The dining tilt is a place that never, EVER seems to get warm no matter how I try to keep the fire in there.

Sunday, December 17, 1721

Papa said that Mama and I should be his "critics."

Mama said, "William, words fail me. There is nothing I can say."

I do not think she meant this in praise but Papa's face went bright with pleasure. He rushed off to write again.

Katherine and I had a most interesting discussion about praying. She says she has beads to do it and the beads are called a "rosary." Katherine is worried because in all this time she has not been able to go to Mass. This is like Communion in our church, which she says she could not take from Reverend Jacobs's hands.

I told her I could not take it either. For a different reason. Although I am sure I will be able to start my confirmation lessons as soon as I return to Deer Park. Katherine said in her church I would have had my First Communion "ages since."

Katherine is also worried about Confession. At first I did not understand about it. Then I remembered about the prayer that is headed General Confession and that begins "Almighty and most merciful Father we have erred." I offered to fetch my prayer book so we could say it together but she looked shocked.

Here is a strange thing. In her church — which she calls the Holy Catholic — everything is in Latin. I asked her how she understood it. She said understanding is not what matters most.

P.S. The snow that fell two days ago is still upon the ground.

Tuesday, December 19, 1721

Peg's baby is coming!!! Peg's baby is coming!!! Aengus ran to fetch Katherine back early this morning. I wanted to go with her but she said I could not. The coming is taking a LONG, LONG TIME. Sometimes I have heard Peg calling out and sometimes I have been frightened. All day I have been trying to do Katherine's work as well as I might.

Wednesday, December 20, 1721

Peg's baby is BORN!!!!!! She is a little girl just as Peg wanted. I have been to see her and held her. Even if she did not wake up. It was Aengus who came to tell me. As soon as it was daylight he knocked upon my door. I could not stay long because Katherine sent me back that I might prepare Mama and Papa's breakfast. Papa was not very interested although he mumbled something about "a new birth in a new land." Strangely, I think

Mama was. She asked me how big Peg's baby is and I showed her by holding out my hands.

I have not put before about how the tilts of Katherine and Eamon and Peg and Aengus have been made comfortable and how there are "bits of furniture" there as well.

Thursday, December 21, 1721

I did not know that a baby would cry so much and so loudly. Peg seems worried about the crying but Katherine says she has a sister who was much, much worse. I also did not know that a baby would smell. Or that under the clothing it had to be "swaddled" — just like Jesus. Swaddling means being wrapped up tightly with a long, long band.

I have been neglecting Tibbles so I am giving her some extra strokes.

Friday, December 22, 1721

The baby has a name!!! She is called Mairie, which is like Mary but not quite the same, so I have spelled it differently. Mairie is after Peg's mother, but she is also called Sophie after me. I long to tell Mama and Papa but I do not think the news would please them.

Katherine says having a baby so close to the time

of the Blessed Saviour's birth is a sign of good fortune. I am thinking about the Saviour and how He was born in a manger. And how He came to bring us joy. I feel joy IN ABUNDANCE. I hope Old Lige knows about the baby. I believe that he does.

Babies make lots of washing. This is not easy because it means heating so much water. Katherine and I must do it all because Peg cannot yet get up.

Sunday, December 24, 1721

Katherine tells me she is concerned because Little Mairie cannot be christened. She says Little Mairie's soul is in danger. If she should die she would have to go to Hell and there be burned in flames.

I said I did not think that God could be so cruel because the not-being-christened is not Little Mairie's fault. Katherine said it makes no difference. Little Mairie will at least have to go to Purgatory. I offered to ask Papa if he would read out the Christening Service for them. Katherine says a priest is needed and no one else will do.

I want to pray that Little Mairie will not die but will stay healthy always. But sometimes when Katherine talks of such matters it seems she believes — because I am an Anglican — my prayers may make it all worse.

Little Mairie is so small. I remember Nanny saying God sometimes takes the good back quickly. And Little Mairie cannot be anything else.

Monday, December 25, 1721

Katherine killed two more of the chickens. She cooked everyone a special dinner. Although we did not eat all together, of course. We did not do any of the things we would do on Christmas Day at Deer Park but that was not important. What was important was that Little Mairie had opened her eyes and looked up at me. And I had looked down at her.

I have thought and thought about the Baby Jesus and how maybe a tilt is a little like a stable. Also how I am pleased that even if we do not have shepherds and wise men to come visiting we do not either have Herod the cruel, wicked, killing king.

Tuesday, December 26, 1721

I think that Eamon is angry because Little Mairie bears my name. He scowls at me even more. He does not come into Peg and Aengus's tilt when I am there.

Peg and Katherine keep trying to decide whether Little Mairie looks like Peg or Aengus. I do not think she looks like either of them. She looks like herself. Although she does have Aengus's black hair.

Mama had Katherine bring Little Mairie to see her. I had a terrible time because, all of a sudden, I thought how Little Mairie was wearing part of one of Mama's gowns. I grew very worried, but Mama did not notice so all was well.

How is it that Mama and I are so different? How can Mama not want to take Little Mairie in her arms? I would hold her all day and all the next day and all the next day also. Except that then Katherine would have no one to help her with all the other work.

Peg gets up a little but she is still weak. Katherine says Little Mairie wakes in the night and has to be fed then. She says that is tiring. I expect it is. The way Little Mairie feeds is from Peg's breast. That is another thing I have found out. I know it is not polite but it does make me think of Bessie and her calf. Sometimes the words in my head come pounding. Sometimes I do still so much long to ask how Little Mairie got out.

Sunday, December 31, 1721

I am thinking about what Captain Jones told me about how December 31 is the end only of the "historical year." Katherine says she has never heard of such a thing. But then I had not either. And anyway I wonder if it has to do with how she is a papist. Captain Jones seems to have hinted that it might.

Katherine says that all she knows is that if they were back in their village, everyone would be gathering to see the Old Year out.

I finished the doll I have been making. Peg let me put it at Little Mairie's side. For once she was sleeping very peacefully. In fact, all day she hardly cried.

Monday, January 1, 1721

I have decided to go on putting 1721 until the Legal New Year. Because I would like to be Legal and doing so seems interesting. I could, of course, use Captain Jones's way of putting both years but I think that I will not.

A great New Year's Day event has taken place. It was Katherine who came up with the idea. She said we should go to the clifftop and welcome the New Year with a fire. Even if Little Mairie had to be wrapped up even warmer and Peg had to be helped.

I think Katherine had already decided that the fire would be so that the cove should have a name and that the name should be Mairie's Cove, "after the first child." Peg and Aengus were very pleased and I was also (although I think that Eamon was not).

Katherine says it means that now we are living "somewhere." Instead of "nowhere." She says, to her, it feels much better. It does also, I think, to me, though if we can christen a cove, why can we not christen a child? Still, I suppose this was not really a proper christening, it was just us.

Anyway, I have made myself a promise. The promise is that I am going to speak to Captain Jones about this as soon as I see him. So he can write Mairie's Cove on his chart.

Tuesday, January 2, 1721

Mairie's Cove

I do like writing that we have a name now. Although I do not think I will tell Papa and Mama about it. Mama would not care. But I suspect Papa would be most unhappy. He would perhaps want a name that had more to do with him. That is a mean thing to write maybe, but I am sure that it is true.

P.S. I will not write the name on every day. It takes too long.

Wednesday, January 3, 1721

Peg came with Little Mairie. She said it is time she was up and about again. She cannot keep home anymore. I am sure Little Mairie SMILED at me although Katherine said it is probably only "wind." "Wind" is another thing babies seem to have lots of. The wind must be "brought up" by rubbing them upon the back. They make great belches. This is a word which causes me to think of Mistress Tyler because BELCH was certainly NOT a word she would have approved of having me set down.

As I watch Peg, I do wonder what happened when I myself was small. I remember Nanny speaking of how I had a "wet nurse" to feed me. I did not know what she meant at the time but now I understand it to be someone who was not Mama but who was hired to give me milk. Almost at dinner I was tempted to ask Mama about it but then she looked at me as if I was not sitting properly and so I did not.

Mama has started a picture which has Little Mairie in it. I suppose that is why she wanted to see her. I think Mama is rendering Little Mairie's face quite well.

Tibbles did not seem pleased to have Little Mairie here AT ALL.

Thursday, January 4, 1721

We are trying to get Bessie to eat spruce boughs but she does not like them. Katherine shakes her head.

It continues very cold. Sometimes the cold is all I can think about, and then I am colder still.

Friday, January 5, 1721

Katherine says there is not enough greenery left. Bessie will have to be slaughtered because the hay is almost gone as well. The very idea of killing Bessie makes me sad.

Katherine has decided that goats may be "more what is wanted" for the beginning years. I do not know about goats but I do see how much a cow must eat and I know that already — because we cannot feed her enough — Bessie is giving almost no milk.

Saturday, January 6, 1721

The slaughtering is done. This time I did see a little of it although I could not bear to watch the killing. That would have been TOO MUCH. Bessie's skin has been scraped and saved, for Katherine says it will be useful. Katherine and Peg and Eamon and Aengus discussed as to whether the meat should be salted. They were troubled because they were sure the salt we have here would not be enough. Then Katherine laughed. She said she reckoned the salting would not be needed. If the weather should continue as it has been, the meat will stay "well froze."

I had wondered who the meat would belong to. Katherine says it was "in the bargain" that it would be shared. She says, even she could not "presume to hope" to have this year's cow and chickens and next year's as well.

Monday, January 8, 1721

Katherine has a bruise on her forehead. She insists she banged herself getting wood in, but I do not think that this is true.

Tuesday, January 9, 1721

I was right about Katherine's bruise. Today she was more honest. She told me Eamon hit her because he is jealous. Mostly he is jealous because she loves Little Mairie. And because she talks so much to me!!!

She will sleep with me in the cooking tilt. She has told Eamon she will not live with him any more unless he puts a stop to his "old nonsense."

I am sorry that she is troubled, but as I look across at her I know how much I like having her here still when usually I am by myself.

I think the temperature is even lower. There is ice beneath the door.

Friday, January 12, 1721

Peg came again. She was crying. She said Eamon is "at her and at her" to get Katherine to come back. Katherine said "too bad for the likes of him." But then I went outside and found that Eamon had been listening. I was frightened. He had such a look of anger on his face.

I want to go to Papa. I want to tell him he must stop Eamon waiting by the tilt door in this fashion. Katherine says I must not do this. She says things are bad enough already without her "losing her post."

Saturday, January 13, 1721

A TURMOIL! A TERRIBLE, TERRIBLE TURMOIL! Eamon ENTERED into Mama's tilt. "'Tis you that started this, with your wanting her as a servant," he yelled.

Mama kept quite calm. I cannot imagine how she

did it. She told Eamon he must leave and not return until he could behave in "more seemly fashion." She looked triumphant. As if maybe she was proud of herself. I have to say that I was proud of her.

Sunday, January 14, 1721

I went to Old Lige's grave. I brought Tibbles with me. I said the words that come from the Evensong service: "Give peace in our time, Oh Lord." I suppose they are for wars between countries, but it feels like a war here now.

Tuesday, January 16, 1721

Everything is awful. Peg says she and Aengus have quarrelled also over what should be done. Mostly they just want Katherine to go back to her own tilt and live there.

"Would you have me wait until I am black and blue all over?" Katherine has answered.

I know what I want. I want it that Katherine should be SAFE.

Papa has taken to carrying his gun about with him once more. "To protect us," he says. He stands by the stream with it so that Eamon may not cross. Mama does not believe this is necessary. She says she is certain Eamon has been PUT IN HIS PLACE.

Thursday, January 18, 1721

I do not understand about grown-up people. I found Katherine crying. She says she is LONELY. She says "is not Eamon my husband in the sight of God?" And will she not be "an old maid with never a child to hold" if she does not go back to him?

Suddenly she seems to wish to be returning. I do not want her to go. But I do not want things to be the way they are either. Especially now that I cannot see Little Mairie. That is the WORST OF ALL.

Saturday, January 20, 1721

Once again, it is Mama who has saved us. She told Papa he must summon Eamon to her. I did not think that Eamon would come but he did. Mama has a very commanding presence. She made Katherine and me come also so that we might "stand witness" to Eamon's agreement that his "violence would cease." When he mumbled she made him speak louder.

It is all so strange because afterwards Eamon seemed almost glad for what Mama had caused. Katherine most certainly was. She and Eamon went into the forest together. They waded through the snow to get there. They were gone a LONG, LONG TIME. When Katherine came back she was laughing. She gave me a kiss on the cheek. The kiss was nice. It made me feel as if I were her sister. I had not thought that such a thing could be.

Sunday, January 21, 1721

Eating in the dining tilt grows ever more difficult. Sometimes I think that if we do not eat quickly the food will be frozen to our plates. I can see from how Mama and Papa look so much fatter that we all of us now wear many layers, but after the meal is over we still all leave as soon as we can.

Because it is Sunday I read one of the psalms. It was Psalm 107. The one to which I opened my Bible. It starts out "O Give Thanks unto the Lord for He is gracious." I gave thanks as best I could.

One of the things I should be grateful for is that we all of us seem to have LOTS of under apparel. I wonder if Uncle Thaddeus took a hand in Mama and Papa's packing as he did in mine. I should also be thankful that Mama and Papa have seen fit to put their under apparel on.

Monday, January 22, 1721

Eamon had to bring an axe this morning to break the ice upon the stream. There has been ice before, but always I have been able to get through it myself.

Or there has been a little place that has been open where the water runs fast.

The hens lay very few eggs. I think more of them will be killed quite soon. How clever of Katherine that when the bargain was made that she would work for us, she provided for how the animals might not be able to be kept. She must be very smart.

P.S. Sometimes now Eamon seems almost pleased to see me. Today he even gave me a wink.

Tuesday, January 23, 1721

The sea rages. Eamon and Aengus have pulled the fishing boat up higher so that it will not be washed away.

More snow has come. When I told Katherine how much it makes my toes hurt she gave me rags to wrap around my feet. The rags were made from one of my bedgowns that had worn almost to nothing. They helped a lot. Can it grow even colder yet, I wonder.

Of course, when I lived at Deer Park I was not outside much. But still — even in the out of doors — I do not think it was as cold as here. If I try to hurry too much my chest hurts and my breath seems taken from me. I have to gasp.

Wednesday, January 24, 1721

A RELIEF. Mama has declared that we will eat in the dining tilt no longer. We will eat in her tilt instead. She has summoned Eamon to make the table smaller so that it will fit. The relief is not just that we will be warmer, but that there will be one less fire to keep.

Thursday, January 25, 1721

I do not think Mama is pleased to have us eating in the place that is supposed to be hers, but I do think she is glad to be not so cold. Papa thanked her for her concern for us. She nodded to him graciously.

Papa is getting a little better at tending his own fire, but not so very much. I have to go often to check upon it or I know he will let it out.

I have not put about how we mound the fires up at night so there will be embers that can be blown upon to catch in the morning. This is important. It means that ALWAYS AND ALWAYS there is some heat kept. Papa is not to be trusted for the mounding up at all.

Friday, January 26, 1721

Katherine has been looking at the barrels where the food is stored. She says that although the meat from Bessie and the chickens has made "some fair difference" we must be careful. We cannot go "hog wild."

She and Eamon continue happy. He comes sometimes to be here in the daytime. He fetches water for us. I am even beginning to see why Katherine likes him, for he is very good at jokes.

Today he was being so funny I suddenly burst out speaking in Gaelic. I did not mean to. The words just came. I think I shall try speaking in Gaelic more.

I have chilblains on my hands and toes and ears and they are very itchy. Everyone seems to have them. I saw Papa rubbing at his fingers over dinner and I saw the red and swollen parts. The chilblains are another thing that comes from the cold. I had them at Deer Park also. But not as badly as here.

Saturday, January 27, 1721

Papa saw some white birds on the ground among the tree stumps. He says they look to him as if they might be the same as he once went after on a shooting party in England. He says those birds were called grouse. Only they were brown. He is most excited that tomorrow "he may go out to gain our provender again."

I do not know how his work is progressing. He has not asked Mama and me to listen to it for a LONG, LONG TIME. Sometimes when I go into his tilt to tend his fire he seems simply to be sitting. Although I suppose he may be "pondering" what next he will write. Mama is always painting. Or drawing. She has found a small blank book such as mine. There she makes sketches. I suppose the book was in her trunk.

Eamon and Aengus went hunting for rabbits but the rabbits seem to have disappeared.

Sunday, January 28, 1721

I read the Evensong service aloud. I read it from beginning to end. Tibbles twitched her ears as if she liked to listen. Perhaps I shall read to her some more.

Katherine says my Gaelic is improving. I speak it with her now A LOT.

Monday, January 29, 1721

We have eaten the birds Papa shot for dinner and they were very good. He shot so many he even sent some "to our poor neighbours." That is how he refers to Katherine and Peg and Eamon and Aengus. I do not know why, for they seem to me to have no less than us.

After he returned he said he had "to record his victory." It is hard with Papa because he wishes to be praised SO MUCH.

Little Mairie has a cold. Peg is worried. Where do colds come from? I wonder. Peg holds Little Mairie to her but Little Mairie cries a great deal.

Tuesday, January 30, 1721

Little Mairie's cold is not better. In fact it is worse. Her nose is all stuffed up and she cannot breathe properly. She is very hot and she has grown very quiet. Katherine has sprigs of cedar smouldering. She says it is not what she would have used "at home" but she must "make trials" of what is to be found. At home she would have made an ointment to put on Mairie's chest.

The burning cedar smells clean. Peg is yet more worried. She speaks of what she would do if Little Mairie were "lost" to her. I had been pushing that possibility from me. We are all of us praying MUCH.

Wednesday, January 31, 1721

I have mentioned Little Mairie's cold to Mama. It has made her start another painting. This time there is not only Little Mairie in the picture, there is Peg as well. Mama sent Peg her "good wishes." I was glad of that.

I am going to pray for Little Mairie some more. It is HORRIBLE to hear her wheezing to get her breath.

Thursday, February 1, 1721

Katherine came in the night. She woke me. She told me Little Mairie's fever had broken and all was well. We went through the darkness together to see her. When I came back, the moon was above me. It was shining on the water. I have decided I would like to know more about the herbs that Katherine uses for healing. After all, it may be the cedar that saved Little Mairie's life.

Friday, February 2, 1721

The weather is worsening. We have had a great deal more snow. When I went to get water my fingers and toes hurt so much I almost cried. Katherine says we will heat little stones now to hold when there is need. Aengus came to shovel a path for us to get to the stream and to what is left of the chickens, and also from tilt to tilt.

I have asked Katherine about the herbs. She says she will "instruct" me in the summer when they grow again. Although so far she has not found so many here. I am going to get into bed because there I will be warmer. Even here, in the cooking tilt, I am chilled right to the bone.

Saturday, February 3, 1721

Papa was perturbed this morning because his ink had frozen. I brought it here to warm it. As soon as it was thawed it wrote just as well. Still, that is a lesson to me to keep mine always near the fire.

I showed Papa how to clap his hands against himself to get the blood more flowing. He was pleased at what he called "this new invention." I hope he will remember to do it often. I think it would be well if Papa and Mama would move about more. I have tried to tell them of it but they do not seem to understand.

Now that Little Mairie is better I see how much she has grown. Peg was right. The clothes she made from Mama's gown will not last for very much longer. Can I ask Mama about it this time, I wonder. Or will I have — again — to be a THIEF.

Sunday, February 4, 1721

I spent much of the day with Peg and Aengus. When Aengus was playing his whistle we could see Little Mairie was listening. Peg was glad. She said it is proof that the fever has not made her deaf, as she has seen happen "more times than once."

She started telling me stories about "the fairy folk" that live in the hills where she and Aengus and Eamon and Katherine come from. She even told me a story about a "changeling child" her mother had seen. I am not sure I believe in fairies although I would like to. I know Uncle Thaddeus would be against it. But might he not be wrong?

The wind is so strong it almost tore the door of the tilt out of my hand when I entered.

I do not know why, but all of a sudden I am thinking about Eliza and the girl of the Beothuks and wondering where they are.

P.S. I hope it was not wrong to be speaking of fairies on a Sunday. I did read from my Bible as well.

P.P.S. We speak now often in Gaelic and English all mixed up together. I do like the feel of the Gaelic on my tongue.

Tuesday, February 6, 1721

Papa has asked Mama to paint his portrait. He says it will be needed "for his epic." In the beginning, Mama was not willing. As I see how the picture is progressing it makes me notice how Papa looks so much older.

He does not look at the picture himself. He says he does not wish to "impose on Mama's vision." Mama has put waves in the background. They are very lifelike and this time they do not seem to be disturbing her AT ALL.

Katherine and Eamon had another quarrel but it was only a small one. Katherine says she thinks it will be "kiss and scratch" with them for the rest of their days.

Saturday, February 10, 1721

Papa went hunting again and he shot more of the grouse birds, whatever they are really called. I asked if I might go with him but he said that hunting is not "women's work." I CANNOT SEE WHY.

When he leaves I am always a little worried that he will get lost in the forest, but so far he has always managed to return. In fact, he does not go very far. Eamon and Aengus have made a path for him. He goes to the end of that. The end of the path is at the place where the grouse birds come.

Papa cannot go farther because the snow beneath the trees is now so deep. Katherine has shown Papa how to wrap rags around his feet also. He makes a great fuss of it. Katherine tells me we must ensure he "keeps at it" or his feet will surely freeze.

Sunday, February 11, 1721

Again Katherine and I fell to talking of our churches. Again she told me how worried she and Peg and Aengus — and Eamon even — are that Little Mairie cannot be baptized. Katherine says she had not realized that she was coming to quite such a "God forsaken, priestless country." She says Eamon and Aengus should have told her. They should have said it would not be like Ireland at all.

Her biggest fear is that they will not be able to "stay and prosper" if they must rely always so much on what the ships will bring. Apparently one of the other things Captain Jones has promised to bring when the *Daisy* returns is seed for vegetables. But Katherine is worried that "the bit of old seaweed" they have put down will not make earth enough to let the vegetables grow.

Again I read from the Psalms. I chose Psalm 150, which is the last one — "Praise ye the Lord." I have never felt this way before but the words caused me to shout almost. My mind was EXALTED. Especially where it says, "Praise him with the stringed instruments and organs. Praise him upon the loud cymbals; praise him upon the high sounding cymbals."

I know that if I had had cymbals I would have crashed them. I hope God does not mind.

Wednesday, February 14, 1721

The last of the chickens is killed. Almost I am glad, for it means I will no longer have to go and feed them. Perhaps that is an awful thing to put. But IT IS TRUE.

I want to scratch my hands off. My chilblains are so horrible. They are worst when I am by the fire where it is warmer, which I must be to cook. At Deer Park they NEVER were as bad as this.

Friday, February 16, 1721

Katherine says we must keep up with the spruce beer brewing. She knows that gathering the boughs is now much harder but she is like Peter. She believes the beer is crucial for our health. It is not easy to remember how the forest was when we first came here and how the trees were once so near. When the

Daisy comes back I suppose the men will have to cut new trees down. This will be good because it will create more open land for Katherine and Eamon and Aengus and Peg to use for their farm.

I wonder if Papa is still thinking of how he will make "a plantation." It is hard to imagine it. I suspect "a plantation" means there would be "real houses." But then I suppose that Katherine and Peg and Eamon and Aengus may mean to live in "real" houses themselves some day.

I wonder where they lived in Ireland. Even now I somehow do not think it PROPER that I should ask them. I think they might not like it. I think they would tell me if they wished that I should know.

P.S. Katherine has been commanded to "do something" with Mama's gowns so that "they may be more convenient." I think this means Mama wishes them shortened so that they do not drag upon the floor.

Monday, February 19, 1721

I have not written for several days because I have felt SO LONELY. I have spent as much time as I could playing with Little Mairie. Her hair is much thicker now and her eyes are much less blue. Playing with Little Mairie is the thing I know that always cheers me. Although this time it does not seem to be working as it should.

Tuesday, February 20, 1721

I went to sit with Mama. I do not know why. I just wanted to. She told me I look pale. I did not stay long because, of course, she was busy with her painting. What is the matter with me? Could it be that I am homesick? That I have been away from Deer Park and Uncle Thaddeus and Nanny for TOO, TOO LONG?

Wednesday, February 21, 1721

Katherine was cross. Perhaps she is homesick also. She chided me over how I had washed the dishes. Usually I would not mind this. Today I wanted to sit on the bed and cry.

Friday, February 23, 1721

I MUST "gather myself up" as Nanny would say.

Monday, February 26, 1721

Too sad to write. If it were not for Tibbles I think that I would DIE.

Tuesday, February 27, 1721

What a stupid thing I put when I was writing yesterday. Of course I would not die. Dying is harder. Have I not seen that? Dying is what happened to the men in the fishing boats and to Old Lige.

I DO NOT want to die. I just want FOR ONCE to stay in bed ALL DAY. I want to not have to worry about anything. AT ALL.

Wednesday, February 28, 1721

Peg brought Little Mairie. She bundled her up and trudged through the snow. As Katherine does each day, of course. Peg said Katherine had told her I was "beset by the black miseries." She made me sit by the fire. She did all the things that I do, so Katherine would have a helper.

She and Katherine would not even let me go to Mama's tilt for dinner. Katherine told Mama I was "poorly." They "coddled" me up. I did not know how to thank them. They said I did not have to. They said that always the womenfolk must look to one another. I had never thought of myself as "a woman folk." Doing so makes me proud.

Thursday, March 1, 1721

The last few days I have been SMILING. Because I keep thinking of the kindness of Katherine and Peg. Also of how the winter is passing and how we are coming into March. Is not March the month when the *Daisy* will set forth?

Katherine chased Eamon out of the cooking tilt with a pan because he teased her. I thought it was funny but I think that he did not.

Friday, March 2, 1721

A storm is blowing in. I do not think, in England, it snows in March ever. I think that it is going to here.

Monday, March 5, 1721

Katherine is staying the night. She is afraid she will not be able to find her way home in the blizzard. Indeed, it is difficult just getting from tilt to tilt. I almost became lost after dinner. The snow blew in my eyes. My eyelashes were frozen together. It was lucky Katherine opened the door at just the right moment so I could glimpse the light.

Tuesday, March 6, 1721

An awful thing has happened. The roof on Katherine and Eamon's tilt has collapsed. Katherine says it must have been from the weight of snow upon it. She says none of them had ever heard of such a chance.

Eamon and Aengus have shovelled the other roofs off but we are all of us frightened. I think the snow on the roofs was taller than I am. Peg says Eamon was lucky to escape with his life.

Wednesday, March 7, 1721

Katherine and Eamon have moved in with Peg and Aengus. All day they have been working to try to rescue what they can. They have to dig and dig. Katherine is upset about it. At least the snow has stopped falling although the clouds continue heavy and the wind is VERY strong.

Thursday, March 8, 1721

This is the WORST PART. Katherine and Eamon have discovered that some of the barrels of food that were in their tilt are broken. Peas and biscuit and meat are spilled. Everything is all mixed up with snow and earth from the roof. Mostly it is all ruined. Katherine says Peg and Aengus will share what they have. And they will all of them do what they can to "stretch it." But I can see that Katherine is not certain there will be enough.

Friday, March 9, 1721

I tried to get Katherine to take some of the food from here. She said it would be stealing and that is what rich folks always think of servants and she would have no part of it. I mentioned about Mama's gown and about how Old Lige gave milk to them when he was not supposed to. She seemed to think that that was different because it was when there was plenty. She said that eating less is what she and "her kind" are used to anyway. What has that got to do with it? Surely it cannot be right.

Saturday, March 10, 1721

The food was all counted out. I know it. Captain Jones told me. And Katherine was concerned even before this. Lately she has been saying that with Bessie — and with the chickens — we were too "liberal." We consumed too much too fast.

I tried to talk to her again. She said I did not understand what I was saying. I DO! I know it means we will have less ourselves, but I do not mind that.

Katherine says she will take only what is given willingly. I will give willingly. But once again when it comes to something REALLY IMPORTANT, what I say does not matter AT ALL.

Sunday, March 11, 1721

I have prayed to God for help. Katherine believes she too is going to have a baby. When she told me I was excited. Even though I could see that she was cross.

"'Tis another mouth to feed even before it's born," she told me.

That troubled me A GREAT DEAL. I do not like it that in the summer Katherine could want to have a baby and now she does not want to have one any more.

I tried to find in my Bible about where God fed the Israelites with "manna from heaven." I could not do so but I did beseech Him that He might have "manna" for us.

Wednesday, March 14, 1721

Katherine was banging the pots again. All day I worried about her. And about the baby as well. I thought to simply eat less myself, but then I thought that there would be no use to that if Katherine would not take what I have made left over.

Tomorrow I am going to do the only thing I can think of that will be USEFUL. I am going to talk to Mama.

Thursday, March 15, 1721

Mama did not want to listen. She was busy with another painting but I would not leave. Because she wished to be rid of me she said I might put together "a package of provisions." I had to explain that "a package" would not be sufficient. She acted as if Katherine and Eamon and Peg and Aengus were wastrels. I told her it was not true. I said to her about Jesus and how he shared the loaves and fishes. She said that was "a miracle." She also said she had hoped for miracles enough in her lifetime to be certain that they do not come.

I know why Mama will not pay attention. It is because she believes that Katherine and Eamon and Peg and Aengus are less important than we are. But I do NOT BELIEVE that. Not any longer. I do not see how it can be.

Saturday, March 17, 1721

I was in despair. I was ready to steal "our" food from out "our" barrels. I was going to force Katherine and Peg and Eamon and Aengus to take it. I did not care about anything except that they and Little Mairie and the baby that is coming should have what we have. Whatever that may be.

Mama summoned me to her. She told me I must make a list. I wanted to ask why but I did not do so. The list is of all the food we have in the cooking tilt and of all the food Katherine says they have as well. It is almost finished. Tomorrow Mama says I must take it to her. I cannot be certain she has changed her mind but perhaps I can hope.

Sunday, March 18, 1721

Mama made me do sums. The sums had to do with how many days it may be until the *Daisy* returns. The days had to be divided into the amounts of everything we have to eat. I was glad that I could still remember how to do it. But when all the sums were finished I was frightened. Have I not done enough cooking now to know how much we usually will use?

At dinner Mama told Papa we must be "practical." We must recognize we are outnumbered and that his gun may not be of much use "in saving us from harm." I wanted to cry out that it is wicked to think that Katherine and Eamon and Aengus and

Peg would ever come against us. But then I thought of how, even now, Eamon still looks VERY, VERY ANGRY sometimes.

Mostly I knew I did not care about Mama's reasons. Even if they are UN-CHRISTIAN and UN-CHARITABLE. As long as what she is planning is for the good.

Monday, March 19, 1721

It is all worked out. Some of the food that will now belong to Eamon and Aengus and Katherine and Peg has been moved to the other side of the stream. Not all of it, because some is in barrels that will be divided at a later date.

Katherine and Peg are most pleased, though Aengus and Eamon are more doubtful. Even Aengus has said he came here so that he would not ever again have to go like a beggar "cap in hand." However it may be, Mama has been thanked for her generosity and Papa as well.

I have gone to Old Lige's grave under the snow and I have made a vow. The vow is that if ever I should get back to Deer Park I will treat EVERYONE all the same.

Also I have prayed much for the *Daisy* because I believe that by now she will have sailed.

Katherine is wondering if it is possible to cook seaweed. She says she believes she has heard of how it may be mixed with flour and fried in little cakes. She is going to try it out tomorrow — though not on Mama and Papa.

Tuesday, March 20, 1721

The seaweed tasted fine. I told Katherine that I was certain if I said to Papa that it was "yet one more example of our vicissitudes," he would down it with relish. I was right, but he was not as enthusiastic as he has usually been about such things. A little I am worried about him. Now when I go to his tilt I find that often he seems to be in despair. I have asked him to read me some of his writing but he will not do so. I do not think this to be a good sign.

I have had to tell him and Mama that we must be more careful with the candles. I do not think he can understand this. I think I will have to take to doling them out.

I believe, however, that Mama considers me differently since I went to her about dividing the food up. I believe she thinks I am more grown up. I asked her to give me one of her gowns for Little Mairie and she agreed to it. I felt a trifle guilty about how I had taken a gown already, but somehow it did not trouble me too much.

Friday, March 23, 1721

Could it be that the weather is warming? When I went to the stream, the sun was shining. I thought that truly I could feel its heat upon my back.

Sunday, March 25, 1722

I almost forgot about LEGAL New Year but then I remembered. Surely if I may now put 1722 "legally" — which I found out about when I was already on the *Daisy* — then I can know that the *Daisy* MUST be on her way.

Tuesday, March 27, 1722

Here is something I have discovered. To have less food on one day is much easier than having less several days in a row. Sometimes I find my stomach is hurting. I do not like that AT ALL. I also do not like it that when I get up from dinner I am still hungry. And that my arms and legs seem heavier to move about.

Papa looks at the food on his plate as if it were just another of his "challenges" but Mama begins to seem worried. The gums in Papa's mouth bleed sometimes. Katherine says this is because he WILL NOT drink his spruce beer.

Thursday, March 29, 1722

Katherine is sick. It has to do with the baby coming. Mostly it means that she keeps bringing up. That would be bad enough, but Tibbles has disappeared. I have not seen her for two whole days.

Aengus says that perhaps a fox has caught her. I miss Tibbles and MISS HER. I WANT HER BACK.

Friday, March 30, 1722

Katherine could not come to work at all and Tibbles is still gone. I wanted to go and beg Katherine to get better, but how can I? I know she would come here if she could.

Saturday, March 31, 1722

Tibbles has been gone such a small while but already the mice grow bolder. I think perhaps there are rats also. I have found holes in some of the food barrels. Losing food is awful but there is nothing I can do.

Monday, April 2, 1722

Mama has noticed Katherine's absence. She asked me about her. I told her I do not know when Katherine will be able to return.

Mama looked at me sharply. She gathered up her skirts and came to the cooking tilt. She watched what I was doing. She seemed to think it was A LOT. I said it was no more than usual. Only Katherine and I would usually do it together. Mama looked at me and looked at me. Then she went away. I would be wondering what is happening to her. Except that I am too tired.

I was right. The weather does grow warmer. But that makes the snow so wet and slushy. The floor of the tilt begins to be mud.

Tuesday, April 3, 1722

Mama decreed that Papa should carry the food to the dining table from the cooking tilt. She said that she will lay the table. I thanked her. Each task less does make some difference, even if it is not much.

Katherine continues sick. I went to see her. I could not stay long, of course, but I did stay long enough to play with Little Mairie. I like how now she reaches out to take things. I am surprised that she puts everything into her mouth.

Wednesday, April 4, 1722

Could it be that because of being hungry Mama is changing? She came to watch me working yet again. She even tried to help a little. I thought I saw that there were tears in her eyes when I was bringing in the water. She called me Sophie instead of "child."

She sent Papa hunting but he came back with nothing. Eamon came to say that they might hunt together. He has come upon an animal that lives in the stream that runs into the head of the cove such as he has never seen before. It lives beneath a pile of sticks and he has found no way to trap it. He will take Papa there tomorrow, but he says they will have to be patient, for the animal only comes out now and then.

Thursday, April 5, 1722

Eamon and Papa were unsuccessful. Katherine is sick still. She does not bring up any longer but she seems to be weak. She cannot walk well because her ankles are very swollen. I have asked her if there is some herb that I might get her. She says she knows none in this place.

I wish I could stop thinking of Deer Park and all we ate there. And all that I think must have been thrown away.

The time goes by so slowly. I had believed that when the days grew longer it would be easier, but it is not.

Still, really the snow is going. Today, in a place where the wind had swept the snow clear, I saw a patch of earth.

Friday, April 6, 1722

The weather was dark and we had to light the candles early. I cannot write more because the one I had set out for today is almost done.

Saturday, April 7, 1722

Rain.

Monday, April 9, 1722

Something AWFUL has happened. With the rain and the melting snow, water fell on Papa's papers in the nighttime. I tried to help him rescue them, but even as we touched them they clumped into a mass within our hands. I did set some to dry, but the ink had run on them. The words cannot be made out any longer.

Papa stayed in his tilt all day. He would not come out even for dinner. I tried to bring him something to be eating but he had barred the door.

Tuesday, April 10, 1722

Papa says he cannot start over. But his poem was the whole purpose for us BEING HERE.

I have offered to tear some pages from my book to give him. He has refused them. I do not understand.

Wednesday, April 11, 1722

Papa seems almost relieved. Mama does also. How can this be?

Thursday, April 12, 1722

I opened a new barrel of biscuit and I found these little grubs. I went and asked Katherine and Peg what I should do. Peg said the grubs would float to the surface when the biscuit was soaking. I could skim them off then. I was very relieved to find I would not be caused to throw the biscuit out.

Saturday, April 14, 1722

Katherine has returned to work. She will not have a baby. She says she has "miscarried" also. Her face is thin and she looks SAD.

Sunday, April 15, 1722

I prayed for the *Daisy* and "all who sail in her." I know it is too soon, but I find myself looking towards the water often. I want to see her there SO MUCH. Papa came to sit in the cooking tilt. He suggested Katherine sing for him but she did not.

Katherine says she thinks we must have missed Easter. That is awful. But Easter was not marked on my calendar so how could I have known?

Tuesday, April 17, 1722

On the beach I picked up some dried seaweed. Before I knew it I was stuffing more and more of it into my mouth. I did not care what it tasted like. I just swallowed it down.

Sunday, April 22, 1722

When I prayed this morning it was that Thomas would forgive me. Perhaps, however, if he knew of our difficulties he would feel some sympathy for us. Papa calls our time here "a brave attempt." I wish he would not. I wish he would say he was sorry for making us come, but I think he does not see things in that light. I keep expecting Mama to be angry with him. But today she said, "Poor William."

Almost it is as if she might have sympathy for him. I am very surprised.

I am also surprised that Mama now goes abroad to do her sketching. And that she has made pictures of Katherine and Eamon's fallen down tilt.

Monday, April 23, 1722

How can I explain what happened? I cannot. I just know that I heard Aengus playing his whistle and Papa was by the door of the cooking tilt and I took his hands and began to dance with him towards the stream. When Aengus saw us he played louder. Everyone else came. Katherine and Eamon danced together. Peg danced with Little Mairie in her arms. Mama stepped out to see us. She even clapped her hands.

"'Twill help to keep us going," Katherine said, when we could dance no more.

P.S. Could it be that St. George was giving us strength — even if some of us are not English? After all, as I suddenly remember, it is his day.

Tuesday, April 24, 1722

PRAISE GOD! A seal entered the cove. It lay upon the beach. Aengus came quietly to tell Papa of its presence. Papa got ready VERY QUICKLY. He shot it. Seal meat is very oily but the oiliness is GOOD!!!!

Wednesday, April 25, 1722

The seal meat is a relief to all of us. Although I think perhaps I ate too much. Katherine said we should "be sparing" but we could not be so. Almost I wanted to eat the meat before it was cooked. Peg says she hopes it will be good for adding to her milk for Little Mairie, for she has been worried about that. There is much seal meat left still. Aengus says "we shall not want for another seal as long as the *Daisy* do be coming soon."

Thursday, April 26, 1722

I have checked back in my writing so that I might tell Eamon and Aengus on what day the *Daisy* made land last year. They have begun keeping watch from the clifftop. They have lit a fire there so that the *Daisy* will know where to come. I saw a bird that is like a robin. Oh please, please, let the *Daisy* hurry. Oh, dear Almighty Father, please let her not be wrecked.

Saturday, April 28, 1722

The *Daisy* has been sighted. I have gone to the clifftop to see her. She is trapped in the ice. Eamon and Katherine and Peg and Aengus and Papa were all of us waving and shouting. Mama came up to be with us. All of a sudden I realized that she was shouting as well. I have never heard her do that in such fashion. NOT EVER, EVER BEFORE.

Sunday, April 29, 1722

The *Daisy* remains trapped. We all of us grow more fearful. I can hardly bear to watch for I remember how Captain Jones said a ship could be "crushed to splinters." I wish I did not know what I think will happen if the *Daisy* cannot reach us soon.

Monday, April 30, 1722

The *Daisy* was freed in the night but there is no wind, so she is moving slowly. Could it be that she might be blown back again? That her breaking through the ice might be some cruel joke?

Tuesday, May 1, 1722

Oh lovely, lovely Captain Jones and Mr. Chivers. Oh wonderful Aaron and Silas and Rowlie and Jim and Peter and Jack. Oh, dancing, dancing May Day. Oh, praise, praise God that "those on land and those that have voyaged by sea" are SAFE.

That is the prayer that Reverend Jacobs said when the fishing boat had come for us and we had gone out upon the *Daisy* and everyone had finished crowding round. Reverend Jacobs got up onto the poop deck with Captain Jones beside him. He made everyone bow their heads.

I have not prayed with more joyousness in all my life. Some of that had to do with how Thomas had come to stand by me.

At first I did not know what to say to him, but it turns out his grandmother had had "a premonition" because Old Lige had come to her in a dream. He had come in a dream to Thomas also. He had told Thomas to stop being angry and to be good to me. Thomas had known that this was something he must do. He looked most concerned when he first saw me. I suppose truly I was a sight. In fact, I saw a look of shock on other faces besides. There was shock for seeing the state of Mama and Papa and Katherine and Eamon and Aengus and Peg as well.

The *Daisy* has a new surgeon. I do not know his name yet. I just know that he has said that tomorrow he will examine us and check our health. I think that this is a good thing but today, already, I feel better. We had dinner with Captain Jones in his cabin. We had as much as we could eat. Captain

Jones said I might get sick if I was not careful, but I did not. And I ate A GREAT DEAL.

For dinner, I dressed myself in the new clothes and shoes that Uncle Thaddeus had sent me. The new clothes felt so lovely. They are even the right length. Although they do make me realize how thin I have become.

P.S. Something else to be glad of. The *Daisy* has ANOTHER CAT!!!

Wednesday, May 2, 1722

Thomas and I went to stand by Old Lige's grave awhile. Both of us were very sad. We spoke of how there is no one who knew him who has not said he will be "greatly missed." And how many have shed tears.

Captain Jones talked much of how Uncle Thaddeus has worried for us. How he has said over and over he feared we must have "met our deaths."

Captain Jones has not asked Papa about his writing and Papa has not mentioned it. Neither has Mama.

Papa is pleased because Captain Jones makes much of the fact that we have survived here. Tomorrow I shall go to Captain Jones and tell him of all that Eamon and Katherine and Aengus and Peg have been to us. I shall ask him to help them as much as he can.

Thursday, May 3, 1722

I spent some time sitting in the sun. Mr. Atwood — the new surgeon who has replaced Mr. Yonge and who is very handsome — insisted upon it. He said that all of us must "rest much." I think that this is what I wish to do.

There was a great deal to see and hear because, as I foresaw, the work of rebuilding has all been begun again. The stages and the flakes and tilts are being readied apace. Even with the work, Thomas had time to come to see me. He says he will go out with the boats this year. He will be "midshipman" and Rowlie will be "master" and Silas "foreshipman." Thomas is very excited about it, although he was most careful to say also he would not wish his grandfather lost to him "for all the sea-going in the world."

He told me Joshua was "brought before the magistrate" for poaching, so Captain Jones would not have him aboard. I said I was not sorry. Joshua was not someone I wanted to see EVER AGAIN.

It is lovely to hear the Dorset way of speaking once more — Old Lige's way. Although, of course, I do like Eamon and Katherine and Peg and Aengus's Irish way as well.

The men make much of Little Mairie. Especially Silas. He takes her to hold a lot. I have told Captain Jones the cove has been named after her and he has said he believes that to be "fitting."

A new Irish woman has come. Her name is Nuala and her husband's name is Micah or Mike. They too will stay at the end of the season. It seems then that there will truly be a plantation here, whether Papa has started it or not.

Friday, May 4, 1722

It is Ascension Day. At least I can celebrate that. We had a PROPER service. With hymns and Reverend Jacobs reading the prayers from the prayer book. Reverend Jacobs says he is certain God will forgive me about Easter if I will read the story of it over. I should have thought of that myself, of course. I hope God will forgive me that I REALLY, REALLY was too tired.

Saturday, May 5, 1722

I am confused. I had thought that Mama and Papa at least would go back to living on the ship. And perhaps I would have to go as well. Captain Jones has offered, but Mama has said she does not wish "to return to its confines." She has, however, organized it so that meals will be brought to us. And she has said that we should start to eat in the dining tilt again. And Captain Jones may be OUR guest.

Eamon and Aengus are working with the other men now, of course.

Katherine tells me her "agreement" with us is over. She and Peg work in their garden whenever there is a moment. Captain Jones did bring the plough and the seeds for the vegetables (as well as the new clothes). The seeds are for carrots and turnips and cabbage. Katherine and Peg want everything ready for the planting. I shall help them as much as I can. That way I will not miss Katherine quite so much.

Sunday, May 6, 1722

The new cat begins to come to me. She is much friendlier than Tibbles was at first.

Captain Jones says that now I am "somewhat recovered" I may have the gift that Uncle Thaddeus sent me. It is a violin — or as the men would call it, "a fiddle." I asked him what Uncle Thaddeus had intended that I might do with it. Captain Jones said merely that Uncle Thaddeus was "very distracted" at the *Daisy*'s departure and so he did not know.

Tuesday, May 8, 1722

Another ship has come. It is called the *Martha* and it has landed across the cove. Captain Jones says that now he must "play the admiral" and keep order. Always, whoever is the captain of "the first ship to the fishery" must take charge.

Mama paints and paints. Even sometimes the men. She does not make them stand still. She works quickly. And she makes their movements seem alive. Sometimes she lets me watch her. And sometimes she seems almost happy in what she does.

Mama and Papa do not need fires all the time any longer. When they do, Jack sees to it. Which is another great relief.

Wednesday, May 9, 1722

Some of the *Martha*'s men rowed over to boast about how they will catch more fish than the men of the *Daisy*. They SCARE me. As our men do not.

I thought I should try playing Uncle Thaddeus's violin — his fiddle — but then I saw that Thomas was carrying spruce branches and so I went to help. Thomas teased me about how when we came here I could hardly lift a single twig. I told him I had thought of that myself. He said that now I "be a lady of strength." We looked at each other and laughed.

Friday, May 11, 1722

I hope Uncle Thaddeus will not mind but I have given the fiddle to Papa. I feel he has need of it since he cannot be writing any more. He was delighted and began trying to play it at once.

Sunday, May 13, 1722

I spoke to Reverend Jacobs about being confirmed. He says it cannot be done here for there is need of a bishop. Still, he will begin to instruct me. We started on the Catechism of which I know something from Mistress Tyler. I spoke to him also of the needs of Katherine and Peg and Eamon and Aengus. For Mass and for Confession. He told me he can do nothing "as to that."

Monday, May 14, 1722

The stage head for the *Daisy* is built again. The other two are also almost done. Katherine and Eamon's new tilt is ready for them to move into. Eamon even invited me to go to look at it. Thomas came with me. He talks to me now more freely. I am glad to say that Little Mairie likes him almost as much as she likes me.

It is lovely to have a cat to sleep with me once

more. I have named her "New Cat" because the name seems right.

Tuesday, May 15, 1722

The animals were fetched out. There is another cow and more chickens. I have been pleased ever since I saw them. What if they had not been brought for some reason? What if our bargain with Katherine could not have been kept?

The pigs Katherine had told me of were unloaded also. As well there are some GOATS. Captain Jones said he thought much upon the matter. He believed goats would serve better than another calf and there was enough of Eamon and Aengus's money to pay for them. Katherine smiled much.

Papa says Mr. Robinson Crusoe had goats. Perhaps that does not matter now.

Wednesday, May 16, 1722

I have told Peter I will search for eggs again if he should wish it. He DOES.

Friday, May 18, 1722

It is hard to know what to put for so much of what is happening is the same as happened before. I do not want to tell of it all over. I will say then only how happy I am to be amongst all this busyness again.

Sunday, May 20, 1722

More studying of the Catechism with Reverend Jacobs. I shall be glad, I think, that Mistress Tyler gave me so much practice in learning things by heart.

Tuesday, May 22, 1722

Captain Jones came to sit by me and speak to me about Uncle Thaddeus. I asked him for news of Nanny but he has none. He says it is "not the sort of matter" men discuss. He says that although Uncle Thaddeus has been worried he is well and "his fortunes prosper." I told him I was glad for that.

Thursday, May 24, 1722

Everything is AWFUL! AWFUL! I am so, so disturbed!!!!

The Beothuk people came back. Before they could leave, the men from the *Martha* saw them. The men from the *Martha* jumped into their fishing boats and set to chase the Beothuk people off. The

captain of the *Martha* came to our beach. He insisted to Captain Jones that such "savages" should be
got rid of. He told Captain Jones he has guns and he
is going to issue them and the rest of his men may
fight with knives.

Captain Jones ordered him to desist. The captain
of the *Martha* would take no notice. All evening his
men have been laughing and singing. Aaron says he
believes that they are drinking rum.

Captain Jones is very firm. He has said that if any
of the *Daisy*'s men leave "on such an errand" they
will not be "welcome to return." But there are those
that are in doubt. Even Jack. Even Rowlie and Silas.
And Katherine and Peg and Eamon. And Aengus,
who says they must "look to the safety of their
homes."

When I saw the Beothuks I called out and ran
towards them. I wanted to see the girl again. I think
I even glimpsed her. I am afraid that somehow it is
my fault that they came here. I hate the sound of the
shouting that is GROWING AND GROWING from
across the water on the other side.

Friday, May 25, 1722

The men from the *Martha* left with the dawning.
I saw them because I had not slept a wink. All I can

think of is to pray to God that the Beothuk people went so quickly they are now FAR, FAR AWAY.

Saturday, May 26, 1722

The men from the *Martha* came back with blood upon their clothing. They called our men cowards. I can only fear the worst.

Sunday, May 27, 1722

The men from the *Martha* claim that they have "gained a great victory." They seem to think that it is funny. They say that there was not one "savage" left alive. Reverend Jacobs said we must pray for their souls "for that they are in need of redemption." Should we not be praying for the Beothuks more?

Monday, May 28, 1722

I am so proud of Thomas. He is the BEST of all of us.

A man from the *Martha* came to bring Eliza to me. He tried to tell me "they wicked folk" must have stolen her. He would not listen to me when I said this was not so.

I could not get it from my head that the girl might still be living. I went to Captain Jones. I begged him that he would send a fishing boat to see. Captain

Jones looked as if he were relieved he might do something. He brought the men together. He called for volunteers.

Thomas stepped forward at once. He spoke about Old Lige. Silas and Rowlie came then to stand with him. I am not sure they had changed their minds quite. I think they were stirred by his example. In a minute Jack and his crew were stepping forward also.

Others would have gone. But Captain Jones said those two boats would be sufficient. Mr. Atwood has left with them in case "his skill in matters medical" might be of use.

Tuesday, May 29, 1722

Thomas says the sight that met their eyes was "dreadful." The others all say that as well. They will not describe it. They say they cannot. But Thomas said it heaved up his stomach so he was sick.

The girl was not alive but a small boy was. They brought him back because he was among the bodies and he was so frightened he could not even run away. Captain Jones has placed him "under guard" in what used to be my cabin. I went to see him but he had hidden himself beneath the bunk and he would not come out.

Wednesday, May 30, 1722

Captain Jones says the work must go on. He is "accountable." I brought food to the boy but he would not eat it. I did not stay with him long for I heard his teeth chattering. I knew he was afraid of me.

Thursday, May 31, 1722

The boy has gone. At first Captain Jones thought someone from the *Martha* had taken him to harm him. But now he says he thinks this is not so. The boy has somehow escaped. Thomas says perhaps he knows how to find "others of his kind" to be with. I pray this may be true. Although I do not truly think it is.

I have taken Eliza and I have buried her by where Old Lige is buried. I have put a cross above her. I know the Beothuks were not Christian people. But I believe that Jesus will care for them JUST THE SAME. Also it seems the most that I can do.

At supper I could not help myself. I told Mama and Papa how upset I am. To my surprise, even Mama said she "regretted this happening." She actually looked quite sad.

Captain Jones says everything is almost ready for the fishing. I DO NOT CARE.

Sunday, June 3, 1722

I know what I put about the fishing but I know also that when Reverend Jacobs was praying for "a successful season" I found myself saying "Amen" with all my heart.

Monday, June 4, 1722

I went into the forest. I stayed there a long time. Thomas came to find me. He brought me to Katherine and she made hot milk for me. She fetched Little Mairie to sit upon my knee. I do not know if it is right or not, but I have love in my heart for all these people. I want that they should gain the things they wish AND NEED.

Friday, June 8, 1722

The capelin return. All say it is a good sign. This year I simply hitched up my skirts, took up a maund and waded out for them. I did remember about Joshua. How GLAD I am that he is not here.

Friday, June 15, 1722

The fishing boats went out. They came back empty but the men are not concerned. They say that truly this must be how "the fish do come within these parts." They will keep going out so as not to miss anything but they will not worry yet.

Wednesday, June 20, 1722

The fishing boats came back laden. Thomas is happy because he believes he did his work "right well." It is strange to see Rowlie at the stern oar but, just as when Old Lige was with them and the fishing was successful, theirs was the boat that was filled and came in FIRST.

I am glad to say that I do not think the men of the *Martha* caught fish in such numbers. Perhaps it is their punishment for doing SUCH BAD AND WICKED THINGS.

Tuesday, June 21, 1722

The blackflies return. I had almost forgotten about them. I hope that they are biting the men of the *Martha* even more than they are biting us.

Monday, June 25, 1722

Mosquitoes come again also.

I asked Captain Jones for some paper because there is hardly any space now in my blank book. He says "of paper there is none." He says Uncle Thaddeus would not send any "for that he was so angry with Papa." Perhaps that is why Uncle Thaddeus sent me the fiddle. But paper is what I need.

Captain Jones says he might spare "a page or two." I suppose that Mr. Atwood and Reverend Jacobs might also. But I had thought to keep writing at least until we arrive at Deer Park once more. A page or two is not enough.

Tuesday, June 26, 1722

How can I simply come to the end of this sheet and put my pen down? But paper is like food. I did not think that food could run out either. And now I know it can.

There will be so much to tell. Little Mairie got her first tooth. She sits up almost. I am certain that soon Katherine will find again that she is going to have a baby. Captain Jones says he believes the captain of the *Martha* is losing his hold upon his men and no good will come of it. Mama is distraught that because of the lack of paper she will soon no longer be able to be painting and sketching. Papa is getting better and better at the fiddle. Thomas comes to see me as soon as he has boiled the kettle for Silas and Rowlie after they have come in off the water. Things and things will happen from this. Even if I wrote my smallest I could not say all of it.

I shall say the thing that matters most to me then. This is that I am NOT the same person that I was when I started writing. Being here has changed me VERY MUCH. Mostly I am glad. But I am not glad for all that has been hardest.

I do not know if it is "the way of the world" as Old Lige so often tried to tell me. I just know I would stop people being hungry and hurting and all things of that nature IF I COULD.

Epilogue

✦

As Sophie was writing those last lines there was something she did not know. Uncle Thaddeus may not have sent paper, but he had sent money. Mama and Papa used this to take passage on the first sack ship that came into Mairie's Cove. Sophie was sorry to leave and wept many tears at the parting but, as ever, she was not greatly consulted.

She expected, of course, that the family would be going back to England, but Mama had other plans. The sack ship put in at Trinity, which was already becoming a more settled Newfoundland community, further to the south. A merchant from Poole who had relocated his business there, and who knew Uncle Thaddeus, expressed his willingness to help. A small house was found. The family disembarked; Mama made all the necessary arrangements and another new life began.

Mama had indeed changed. Through her time at Mairie's Cove she had found something to which she was prepared to dedicate herself. She organized a constant supply of paints and paper and brushes. She wandered the village and seashore. She became especially good at capturing the wildness of winds and waves.

When her pictures were finished she had them

shipped to England, where Uncle Thaddeus arranged for their sale. Her work became quite famous. She kept her identity a secret, however, for in those days it was not considered proper for a woman to be making a living in such a way.

Papa went on being a man of wild fantasies and impossible dreams. For a while he thought to make money from his new interest in music. His fiddling did come to assure him a welcome wherever he went, but that was all. Nonetheless, he remained optimistic. He delighted in his wife's achievements and stayed ever certain that someday he too would find fame.

Both he and Mama continued to leave Sophie much to herself. Mama thought mostly of her paintings, although she did share her feelings about them with her daughter more and more. Papa was so eternally prone to distraction that he could not ever truly be counted upon. By now Sophie was even more accustomed to the freedom all this gave her.

At first she tended to matters of the household. In time, as she went about the community, she saw other needs. When the merchant's bookkeeper proved inadequate to his duties, she remembered her skill at figuring as well as her pleasure in it. Convincing the merchant was not easy, but at last she was allowed to take her place on the bookkeeper's high stool. There she worked diligently, keeping the numbers always in their columns, making certain that all the records were straight.

Uncle Thaddeus continued to send her letters whenever there was transport. Because she asked him to do so, he kept her informed of what he knew of events in Mairie's Cove. She found out that, in that first season, fighting had finally broken out between the men from the *Daisy* and the *Martha*. It was with much difficulty that Captain Jones had been able to gain control of the situation so that once more the season could be brought to a successful end.

What Sophie wanted most was news of Thomas, of Katherine and Eamon, of Little Mairie and Aengus and Peg. Captain Jones returned to Mairie's Cove for many years to follow, but he never seemed interested enough in the doings of those who were closest to Sophie's heart. When she was seventeen she could bear it no longer. By now, through her work as a bookkeeper, she had her own money. With it, she found a sack ship that would carry her. She asked Papa if he wished to accompany her, but when he said that he did not, she once more took matters into her own hands and set off by herself.

When she arrived, it was as if Thomas had been waiting for her. On their first walk together he blurted out that he loved her and had been hoping always for her return. She knew well enough by that time that she loved him. The sack ship remained only a very few days, but by the time Sophie left on it, she and Thomas had agreed that in the following year they would marry and both of them would come to Mairie's Cove to stay.

By then the Cove was far less lonely. The love between Katherine and Eamon still tended to be stormy, but they had two children, both of them boys. Little Mairie had a sister. More couples had come from Ireland, and Jim and Jack had settled also with their wives. Aengus and Peg had built themselves a house to replace their tilt, and Katherine and Eamon and others had followed suit. Farming still produced little, but the work of clearing and cultivating was going on.

Mama and Papa were displeased at Sophie's choice of husband, but there was nothing they could do to make her change her mind. Indeed, they had become so accustomed to her making her own decisions that they did not even argue with her very much.

Thomas and Sophie were the first couple to actually be married in the Mairie's Cove community and it was Reverend Jacobs who solemnized their wedding. Life continued hard and they were not always happy. Thomas was a good and caring husband, but no children came to them and for this they grieved.

Sophie kept finding new ways to be useful. In the winter months she would teach the children "their letters," although classes could not continue in the summer, for then the children had to help with the fishery work. Sophie also fulfilled her wish to learn about healing and herbs, and she put her knowledge to good use.

She corresponded with her parents but she never saw them again. She did not see Uncle Thaddeus either, although she always kept in touch as best she could.

Through all of her life she spoke much of what had happened to the Beothuk people she had met. She did her best to ensure that their memory be kept alive. She wrote letters to the governor of the island, beseeching that he exercise his power to prevent such tragedies from happening again. She died before it became known that the Beothuk and their way of life had been lost forever.

Just as Uncle Thaddeus had predicted, Sophie cherished her record of her first year in the New-Found-Land. In her old age, she passed the pages on to Little Mairie's oldest daughter, who by then had children of her own. The journal was kept safe. It was handed down from one generation to another, along with the doll that Sophie had whittled so long ago.

Historical Note

The era of ships bringing large numbers of men from Europe to fish in Newfoundland during the summers had its roots in events of the late fifteenth century. It all began with the explorer John Cabot, who came across the Atlantic in 1497, bearing letters patent issued by King Henry VII of England. Cabot was authorized to sail to all parts "of the eastern, western and northern sea" to discover and investigate "whatsoever islands, countries, regions or provinces" he might find. Whether he made landfall at Bonavista in Newfoundland or in Cape Breton is a matter of discussion among historians. What is certain is that, on his return, he talked glowingly of the fishing grounds he had found.

News of his discovery spread. By the beginning of the sixteenth century, ships were coming to the fishery from France, Portugal and Spain. Although Cabot's efforts meant that Newfoundland theoretically "belonged" to England, that country was somewhat slower to take advantage of the opportunities offered. The gap was narrowed, however, and before the seventeenth century came to an end Britain was sending at least two hundred ships into Newfoundland waters each season.

The fish sought most eagerly were cod. In a good year the Newfoundland seas seemed to run with them. For the merchants of England they became the means to greater access to both foreign currencies and markets — in salt from Spain; in wine from Spain and Portugal; in molasses, sugar and rum from the Caribbean Islands; in products for sale to and from the developing colonies of New England.

The ports of England's West Country were the usual points of departure. These ports flourished; so did the ports of southern Ireland where the fishing ships stopped to pick up additional supplies. The English economy was also affected by the fact that as many as 10,000 "Newfoundland Men" left their West Country homes each season for the fishery work.

Those who came worked mostly for a share of the profits from the catch. Catches varied. There were good years and poor years. Still, by 1752 the English fishery was exporting as much as 500,000 quintals or 250,000 kilograms of dry cod to its foreign markets for an annual profit of $300,000. Such results led an English politician to declare, in 1784, that Newfoundland "was a more inexhaustible and infinitely more valuable source of wealth than all the mines in the world."

So important was the fishery that Newfoundland was a sought-after prize in the succession of wars between England and other European countries. Not until 1713 was it finally negotiated that the island should belong to Britain "wholly of right." Even then the French maintained fishing rights north of Cape Bonavista. This, in part, explains why in 1721 Uncle Thaddeus and those like him were only just beginning to send their ships to the more northerly parts of the island.

One of the reasons the fishery produced substantial profits was that the Catholic Church insisted that no meat should be eaten on Fridays and holy days. This meant that there were at least 150 potential "fish days" each year. The issue of when fish should be eaten was also something that could be manipulated by governments. England, for example, was officially Protestant. Nevertheless, Queen Elizabeth I declared that an extra fish day should be added to each week — bringing the number from two to three. She also instituted punishments involving a fine of three pounds or three months imprisonment for eating meat on fish days. The express purpose for all this was to ensure an increase in fish sales.

The French tended to ship their catch home "green" or "wet." That meant the fish were headed and gutted and then placed in the ship's hold with large amounts of salt. It was the English who used the process described in *Winter of Peril*. In doing so, they changed the landscape of Newfoundland forever. So great was the need for lumber to make the tilts, flakes and stages that forests disappeared quickly and were never able to regenerate.

The debate over whether Newfoundland should become a place of year-round settlement was fierce. Some insisted that those in permanent residence would harm the merchants' monopoly and therefore their profits. Others saw that money was to be made because those same residents were always in need of supplies. There was concern that, with an increase in permanent residence and a consequent decrease in "Newfoundland Men" coming from the West Country, the British navy would be harmed. This was because Britain did not maintain a large, permanent naval force. The "Newfoundland Men" were experienced seamen. They were regarded as an ever-available resource, ready to swell the navy's numbers in times of need.

It was also claimed that the Newfoundland soil was too thin for farming and the weather too inhospitable. Lobbying for and against permanent settlement continued even after the late 1670s when the Committee for Trade and Plantations in London decreed that those who came to settle should be allowed to stay.

Governments are one thing. People are another. In the end, settlement simply proved unstoppable. Numbers fluctuated and records are not fully reliable. It would seem, however, that the island's year-round population grew from over 2,000 in 1720 to over 3,500 in 1740 to almost 12,000 in 1770. By the early 1800s, immigrants were arriving in substantial numbers. Many came from Ireland, but the West Country still made its contribution, so that both Irish and West Country rhythms and phrases can be heard in speech in different parts of Newfoundland to this day.

Cod — so basic to everything that throughout Newfoundland it is referred to simply as "fish" — remained crucial. Right into the twentieth century the means of catching and "making" changed little, except that it was the women who became responsible for the shore work. There are many people who remember working on the flakes and fishing from the dories. Sophie would have known just how to go on being useful if she had found herself carried forward in time.

The Beothuk form a tragic strand in Newfoundland's history. Even those who have devoted their lives to such studies cannot say exactly why this First Nations people became extinct. Massacres such as the one described in *Winter of Peril* are definitely known to have happened. They do not seem to have been sufficient to account for the death of everyone, however. European diseases were probably a factor. Mostly it would appear that, as the fishery grew and settlers increased in number, the Beothuk no longer had access to the hunting and fishing grounds on which they depended for food.

Certainly, the last known survivor was starving when she threw herself upon the mercy of the white community. Her name was Shawnadithit. She was taken in and cared for. She provided almost all of the firsthand information about her people that still remains. Shawnadithit died in St. John's of tuberculosis in 1829.

Estimates of the number of Beothuk living in Newfoundland before European contact vary from 500 to 2,000. Most experts consider that the lower number is likely to be more accurate. Much archaeological work has been done in the places where the Beothuk are known to have lived. These sites reveal that objects left behind by the fishermen were adapted by the Beothuk to their own needs, with considerable skill. It is thought that by visiting the fishing beaches after the end of the season, the Beothuk were accessing what they saw as just one more available resource offered by the land.

Mairie's Cove cannot be found on any current

map of Newfoundland. Settlements like it would have been among the many "outports" — the remote coastal communities — which were closed in the 1950s out of a wish to give people greater access to opportunities of various kinds. In some cases, houses were floated across the water to their new locations in what were termed "growth centres." The effectiveness of the undertaking was, and is, yet one more cause for debate.

As for the character of Sophie: the behaviour of her parents may seem puzzling. So may her acceptance of it, but she was growing up in a time of very different family circumstances. All children were expected to place obedience and respect for their elders at the top of their list of priorities. The children of the rich were largely raised by servants; parents commonly paid their children little attention and often did not even see them for days on end.

In keeping her journal, Sophie would have been most unusual — as Uncle Thaddeus would have been for encouraging her. Much of learning to write had to do with copying. Women were particularly discouraged from showing their creativity. For them, the keeping of journals was not considered a proper activity until much later in the century. Paper itself was scarce and expensive — quite different as a commodity from now.

Readers today will probably be surprised at the frequency with which Sophie turns to her Bible. But at the time she was living, religion was far more central to everyone's lives. Almost all of the books provided for children were of a religious nature. Indeed, novels were a fairly new form of literature for adults. *Robinson Crusoe* was one of the first to be made available, which is part of why it created such a stir.

Even more surprising to today's reader is the use of different dating systems. In this too, as Captain Jones explains to Sophie, religion played an important part. The calendar used in England, the Julian calendar, had been established by Julius Caesar in Roman times. Unfortunately it worked on a year that was too long according to the actual movements of the sun. In 1582 Pope Gregory XIII introduced the Gregorian calendar. This "corrected" the difference by establishing that the process of reckoning leap years (which give February an extra day in years which are divisible by four) should be altered so that century years would be leap years only if they were divisible by 400.

By Pope Gregory's time, however, religious dissent had sundered the Catholic Church. Protestant countries were reluctant to follow his dictates. This was particularly true of England, which maintained its resistance to his calendar until 1752. At that point, the changeover could only be accomplished by removing nine days from the English calendar for the month of September for that year.

None of this fully explains why new years could begin on different days in different countries — and sometimes, within those countries, on different days in different cities and regions. That also concerned religion, for it was based on the celebration of different events in the life of Jesus Christ. In establishing the Legal or Civil New Year, England used the Annunciation method, which had to do with the day on which it was made known to the Virgin Mary, that Christ was going to be born. Although New Year's festivities always took place in celebration of the turning of the year on January 1, the Legal New Year was appointed as beginning with the Feast of the Annunciation on March 25.

It is through such details that we gain some understanding of the journey we are taking as we follow Sophie's story and step into her world. We see that we are entering a time when to be right according to scientific theory is less important than to be right according to God's law; when travel is so much more laborious that the actual date of happenings may be of minimal concern; when many among the population have no use for calendars because they cannot read them; when, for such people, the sun and moon are the most important tellers of time.

The awareness may bring us a shiver of excitement — and that is what the experiencing of history through the lives of others is all about.

A bodice with stays. Although this one laces at the front, with other styles a helper would be needed to lace the bodice up at the back. The term that would be more familiar to today's reader would be corset.

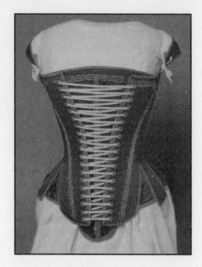

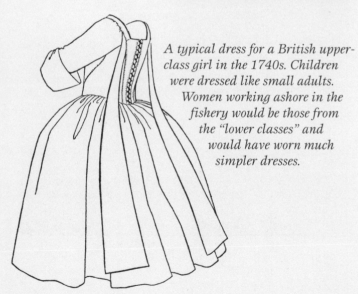

A typical dress for a British upper-class girl in the 1740s. Children were dressed like small adults. Women working ashore in the fishery would be those from the "lower classes" and would have worn much simpler dresses.

An 1897 stamp from Newfoundland, showing John Cabot's ship, the Matthew, *leaving the Avon.*

Cabot in the Matthew *off Cape Bonavista in 1497. It was Cabot's discovery of the huge number of cod in the waters off Newfoundland that spurred the North American fishery.*

Flyboat, an eighteenth-century dry-fishery vessel such as those that the English used in the Newfoundland fishery.

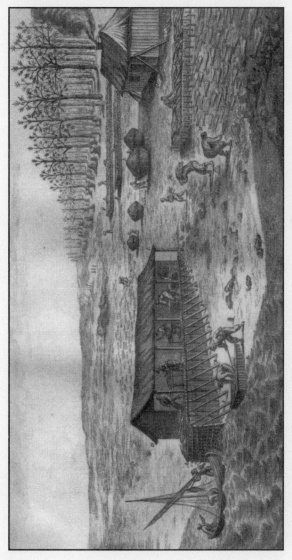

An 18th-century plate showing roofed stages on land, uncovered stages extending to the shore, and drying racks for the cod. A great deal of lumber was needed to build the tilts, racks and stages.

Fishermen went to sea in small boats, then brought the cod ashore to be split, gutted and dried.

The English method of curing the fish was as "dried cod," also called "flat cod." The French shipped cod home "wet" or "green."

Equipment used in the dry-fishery: C small gaff; D baskets for carrying salt; F–I line with sinker, snoods and hooks; T pike; X Large salt shovel; Y small barrels for storing fish oil or salting tongues.

A sketch of an English fishery in Newfoundland.

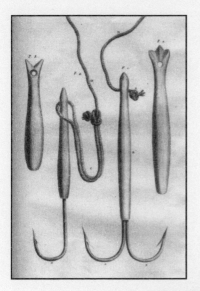

Lures and jigs used for the cod fishery.

Portrait of a young woman named Shawnadithit, the last surviving member of the Beothuk people.

A Beothuk house and canoe, part of a map drawn by John Cartwright in 1773.

Places where the Beothuk are known to have lived, and key European settlements in Newfoundland in the early 1770s. The "location" of Mairie's Cove is approximate, since it was not an actual place, but would have been on the southern end of Notre Dame Bay, east of the present-day town of Twillingate.

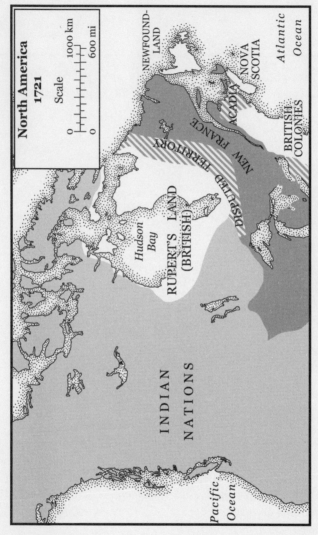

Map of the new world in 1721–1722.

Acknowledgments

✦

Grateful acknowledgment is made for permission to reprint the following:

Cover portrait: Detail from *Children with a Parrot* by Christina Robertson, courtesy of The State Hermitage Museum, St. Petersburg, Russia.
Cover background: Detail (tinted, modified) from "Conception Bay view east," *The Canadian Illustrated News,* courtesy of the National Library, C062634.

Page 202 (upper): © Manchester City Galleries, 2003.109/2.
Page 202 (lower): courtesy of A&C Black Publishers, drawn by S. Gregory, from *Children's Costume in England.*
Page 203 (upper): © Canada Post Corporation, 1897, reproduced with permission.
Page 203 (lower): C. Dinsmore, from J.R. Smallwood's *The Book of Newfoundland,* Newfoundland Book Publishers, 1937.*
Pages 204–207 and 209 (upper): Sketches from Duhamel du Monceau's *Traité général des pesches,* courtesy of the National Library of Canada: Vol II, plate xiv, p. 180; C002505624; C002505623; C002505625; C002505626; C002505627.
Page 208: photograph of a sketch titled *English Fishery at Newfoundland,* held in the Provincial Archives of Newfoundland and Labrador, PANL C1-135.*
Page 209 (lower): *Shawnawdithit (Nancy), the last recorded member of the Beothuk Tribe,* courtesy of the Provincial Archives of Newfoundland and Labrador, PANL A17-110.
Page 210: *A Beothuk house and canoe,* from John Cartwright's map, "A sketch of The River Exploits and The east end of Lieutenant's Lake in Newfoundland" [sic] (ca. 1773), courtesy of the Provincial Archives of Newfoundland and Labrador, PANL MG-100.

Pages 211–212: Maps by Paul Heersink/Paperglyphs. Map data © 2002 Government of Canada with permission from Natural Resources Canada.
Thanks to Barbara Hehner for her careful checking of the manuscript, and to Dr. Shannon Ryan of Memorial University, Newfoundland, for generously sharing his expertise.

*Every effort has been made to locate the copyright holder of the image. Any new information will be included on reprint.

*For Karleen, whose faith in my work
has offered strength and courage,
and who is a friend for all times.*

*Many thanks to Jane Green and Hilda Chaulk Murray
for providing me with accomodation while I was in
Newfoundland for research purposes.
Gratitude in abundance to Sandy Bogart Johnston
for her skilled and thoughtful editing, and for her love
of the task. Also to Diane Kerner for those final
comments which make a world of difference.*

215

About the Author

✦

"I am always somewhat embarrassed when other authors talk about how they spent as much time as they could reading when they were children," Jan Andrews says, "and how they knew they wanted to be writers from the minute they could talk. This is not how it was for me at all. I did love to read, but when there was a choice between reading a book and climbing a tree, the tree climbing always won. I did not even think about being a writer until my children were young and I was making up stories for them. Until then it had never really occurred to me that I might ever have stories in my head."

Even now, Jan admits that she would rather go rock climbing, canoeing, cross-country skiing or hiking than sit at her desk. That has not stopped her producing books that have been shortlisted for major awards, however, nor from creating stories such as *Very Last First Time, The Auction, Keri, Pa's Harvest* and *Out of the Everywhere*, books that have touched readers' hearts across the land. It does not stop her saying, "I love the business of making words work; having them do their job as well as I can manage. I love my working life."

For Jan, writing the story of Sophie Loveridge has

been a particular pleasure because it enabled her go back to her English roots. "I always thought I would never have become a writer if I had not come to Canada soon after finishing university," she says. "And yet, here I am, finding such a delight in re-linking to a part of history that is more especially mine.

"My own ancestors came from the West Country in England. As a child, I used to go on holidays in Dorset. I visited Poole. Loveridge is a family name. Not that my family was ever like Sophie's, as far as I know. My grandmother and my great-grandmother were both servants in other people's houses. If any of my ancestors had been involved in the Newfoundland fishery it would not have been as merchants but as fishermen. Still, I seem to know how Sophie feels and thinks and speaks better than I have done with any other character I have created so far."

The story of *Winter of Peril* goes back a long way in Jan's life. She planned it many years ago and did most of the necessary research, but could never quite find the means to tell the tale. Still, thoughts of what it must have been like to stand on the beach and watch the ships sail away at the end of the season kept returning to her mind. When the opportunity came to make the story into a journal, she leapt at the chance.

Newfoundland is a place where she feels another

connection to her upbringing. For a start, there is the sea, but that is not all. In the course of further research she went to Notre Dame Bay. She heard echoes of those childhood visits to Dorset in the ways of talking. She realized that people were laughing at the quirky things her own family would have laughed at, in just the same way.

As well as being a writer, Jan is a storyteller. She produces a weekly winter series of tellings from the world's great epics and has organized complete performances of *The Iliad* and *The Odyssey* in her own lakeside backyard. She is the director of *StorySave* — a project to record the voices of elders from the Canadian storytelling community for CDs and for a Web site called StorySave.

For Jan Andrews, the stories told and the stories written are vitally important. She believes that through them we gain access to a strength and wisdom that we would never be able to manage on our own. She notes that over the years, Canadian children's literature has changed immensely. More books are being published. They deal in a wondrous array of topics, genres and possibilities for catching at our feelings and our minds. For her, this is a matter of rejoicing. She wants to continue making her own particular contribution to the stories that cannot help but be especially ours.

Library and Archives Canada Cataloguing in Publication

Andrews, Jan, 1942-
Winter of peril : the Newfoundland diary of Sophie Loveridge,
Mairie's Cove, New-Found-Land, 1721 / Jan Andrews.

(Dear Canada)
ISBN 0-7791-1409-4

1. Frontier and pioneer life--Newfoundland and Labrador--Juvenile
fiction. 2. Newfoundland and Labrador--Juvenile fiction.
I. Title. II. Series.

PS8551.N37W55 2004   jC813'.54
C2004-904928-3

6 5 4 3 2 1   Printed in Canada   05 06 07 08 09

The display type was set in Present Bold Condensed.
The text was set in Esprit Book.

✦

Printed in Canada
First printing January 2005

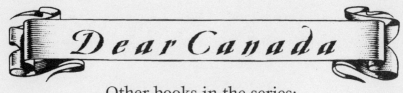
Dear Canada

Other books in the series:

A Prairie as Wide as the Sea
The Immigrant Diary of Ivy Weatherall
by Sarah Ellis

Orphan at My Door
The Home Child Diary of Victoria Cope
by Jean Little

With Nothing But Our Courage
The Loyalist Diary of Mary MacDonald
by Karleen Bradford

Footsteps in the Snow
The Red River Diary of Isobel Scott
by Carol Matas

A Ribbon of Shining Steel
The Railway Diary of Kate Cameron
by Julie Lawson

Whispers of War
The War of 1812 Diary of Susanna Merritt
by Kit Pearson